*To the greatest writer in history, William
 Shakespeare*

Cover: Dynasty Covers

Editor: Pure Harmony Literary Services

Exquisite Reads Publications Presents

A HOOD SUMMER

NIGHT'S DREAM

An anthology of Urban Love Stories

FOREWORD

A Hood Summer Night's Dream is a modern-day ode to William Shakespeare's *A Midsummer Night's Dream*, which is one of my favorite plays. Although the play is classified as a comedy, it is the way Shakespeare's explores the perplexities of love that makes the play so well-known.

Resembling Shakespeare's *A Midsummer Night's Dream*, *A Hood Summer Night's Dream* explores love's perplexities in an enhanced contemporary fashion. The journey begins with finding new love to discovering unexpected love to realizing true, inseparable love to handling dramatic love, this anthology will have you reaching for the Kleenex as tears of happiness, sadness, joy, and relief overcome you!

This anthology also pays homage to Shakespeare's *Sonnet 18*. Everyone has heard the famous line from

Sonnet 18, *Shall I compare thee to a summer's day?* To prevent sounding cliché, I decided to select another sonnet that encompasses the same feelings as *Sonnet 18,* which is Shakespeare's *Sonnet 116.* Below you will find the pleasant paraphrase of Sonnet 116:

Let me not declare any reasons why two
True-minded people should not be married. Love is not love
Which changes when it finds a change in circumstances,
Or bends from its firm stand even when a lover is unfaithful:
Oh no! it is a lighthouse
That sees storms but it never shaken;
Love is the guiding north star to every lost ship,
Whose value cannot be calculated, although its altitude can be measured.
Love is not at the mercy of Time, though physical beauty
Comes within the compass of his sickle.
Love does not alter with hours and weeks,
But, rather, it endures until the last day of life.
If I am proved wrong about these thoughts on love
Then I recant all that I have written, and no man has ever [truly] loved.

Shakespeare is one of the greatest writers in the English language and to complete this anthology in his honor is such a big deal. In high school and college, the question is always asked, *why do we have to learn about Shakespeare? It's not like we are going to need to know about him to get a job.* Well at my schools, the question was asked, but my knowledge of literature has helped me so much as an author. I hope that you enjoy this anthology and maybe even go back and re-read Shakespeare's *A Midsummer Night's Dream.*

Welcome to *A HOOD SUMMER NIGHT'S DREAM! ENJOY!*

Pattie L. Doss

CEO, Exquisite Reads Publications

Table of Contents

ACT I:

New Love

LOVE BEYOND COLOR
PATTI DOSS

"True love cannot be found where it does not exist...nor can it be hidden where it does.
-William Shakespeare

"Hurry up, Logan! I'm ready to get this damn grand opening over with so I can get back home! You know how much I hate being over there. If I weren't the Mayor, I wouldn't be caught dead on that side of town," said James McBride.

Logan rolled his eyes at his father. He hated how his father judged people based on what side of town they lived on. Logan finished dressing and put on his Navy blazer. He had on a baby blue oxford shirt with navy slacks and dark brown loafers. The baby blue shirt matched his eyes and made his eyes appear deeper and brighter.

"Dad, why do you always do that?" He asked his father as he climbed into the black SUV with the tinted windows alongside his father.

"Do what, son?" James asked, slightly agitated.

"Talk down to people from the other side of town. Some of those same people you talk about are the very ones that helped put you in office."

James looked at his son with a terrifying stare and said, "I am a third generation Mayor! I was going to be mayor regardless of who voted!

Logan stared out of the window. He knew his father was right. When it came to politics in the town of Columbus, money ruled over democracy. Votes could be bought, and elections could be rigged for the favorable candidates to win. That's the way it has always been in Columbus and any deserving candidate never stood a chance to clean up the town because almost everybody in government positions was crooked and there was no room for honesty.

The number of candidates that have tried to run based on a platform of honesty was destroyed by mudslinging, lies, and allegations. Things got so bad that honest people stopped running for office and moved away. Not only officials but a majority of the older generations were moving out of Columbus at alarming rates. I guess they felt like going through segregation once in a lifetime was enough and to be constantly stuck in a place that is not growing, while the rest of the world is moving forward was ludicrous.

Secretly, he was praying that his father would not start about him being next in line to run the town. He had no interest in becoming mayor. In fact, he wanted to move as far away from Columbus as he could and open up a car garage and work on cars.

Cars were his passion. He loved everything about them and fixing cars relaxed him in a way nothing else could, but his father hated how much he loved being a mechanic. He felt that being a mechanic was beneath Logan and anyone in the McBride family. He wanted Logan to follow in his footsteps and become a generational mayor of Columbus. Logan did a pretty good job at fooling his dad that he would follow in his footsteps, but in his spare time, he worked as a mechanic for a garage on the other side of Columbus. A side of town his father would never approve of, but Logan loved it. Logan loved interacting with people from different backgrounds and different classes. Being around people other than the rich and snobby, humbled Logan in a way that opened his eyes to issues, he never knew, like how hard middle-class people had to work to make ends meet.

They pulled up to the building of the grand opening. It was a hair salon called *X'Quisite Cuts & Curls*. Logan knew that his father would rush through this grand opening because his father dreaded this side of town, as for Logan, he didn't have a problem because most of his clients from the garage lived on this side of town. As they exited the car, the owner came out to greet them. She was a dark-skinned lady about 5'6, 150 lbs., with hazel eyes. She had on a pair of black ankle pants with white glittered heels with a semi-sheer white sweater and a purple chemise underneath. She was gorgeous, but Logan knew he couldn't even think about talking to her outside of business, as long as his father was around.

His father found out about his love for black girls when he came over and caught his ex-Ashley there. Ashley was a 5'7, caramel-skinned cutie with honey colored eyes that he met at his garage. Her car was making loud noises, and she wanted to see what it was. It ended up being her driver's side wheel barren. Logan fixed her car, and they exchanged numbers. They dated for a while and things were starting to get serious.

One Sunday morning, after Ashley stayed the night. Ashley was cooking Logan breakfast while he was still sleeping. James came over, and Ashley opened the door with one of Logan's Oxford shirts on and nothing underneath. James was pissed and screamed at Ashley demanding to know who she was and why she was there. Ashley and James argued, which woke Logan up. After coming downstairs and seeing his father and girlfriend going at it, Logan tried to intervene, but instead of standing up for Ashley, he asked her to leave and told her that he would call her later. Ashley realized that he would never stand up to his father about his love for her or any other woman of color, so she broke up with him and continued her rant to his father about being a racist, corrupt asshole.

The pain of losing Ashley still hurt Logan and because of it, he put dating on the back burner for a while. Seeing the owner of the new shop, had him rethinking that decision. She was simply breathtaking.

"Hello! I'm Sariyah James, the owner of the shop," the beautiful lady said as she reached out her hand to Mayor McBride to shake.

Sensing his father's hesitation, Logan grabbed Sariyah's hand and shook it firmly.

"I'm Logan McBride. Please excuse my father, but he is feeling a little under the weather, so I will be handling the grand opening if that is okay with you?" Logan stated.

"Miss James, I'm truly sorry. Please forgive me, but my son will take excellent care of you in my absence. I thought I was feeling well enough to attend this event, but I'm afraid I was wrong. I just wanted to tell you in person," Mayor McBride declared and turned to get back into the truck. He looked back at Logan, his eyes telling him not to even think about getting with Sariyah. Logan looked back at him with blank eyes as if he had not heard him or seen the seriousness in his face and turned his attention back to Sariyah.

"Miss James, shall we get this party started?" Logan said holding out his hand to her while flashing her his beautiful broad smile and small dimples.

Once they entered the shop, everybody stopped what they were doing and started staring at Logan as if he had three heads.

"It's okay, Logan. They're cool, I promise. A lot of them are just never around white people, no offense," Sariyah declared.

"None taken. I understand completely. Before I get to enjoy this wonderful party can we go ahead and do the ribbon-cutting ceremony, so the lady from the newspaper can get the picture?" Logan replied.

Sariyah and her staff gathered with Logan behind the beautiful, large purple ribbon that was tied in a bow in the front of her shop. Being that close to her was making Logan nervous. He didn't want her to think he was purposely trying to get behind her, but the photographer kept telling them to squeeze in tight. For a moment, it felt like she wanted him to be all on her because even when she didn't have to, she kept getting closer and closer. By the time they took the picture, Sariyah was so close to him, that he could bend down and kiss the back and side of her neck. Her intoxicating fragrant was driving him nuts, compiled with the way her dress was fitting her; he was trying everything in his power to calm himself before he got a little too excited.

After the ceremony, he handed Sariyah her certificate and congratulated her on her new shop. "Miss James, you have a beautiful shop, and I'm sure you are going to do just fine. Enjoy the rest of your evening."

"Thank-You! Do you need a ride?" She asked him.

"No, I called for a car to pick me up."

"Well, I wish you would have stayed and mingled a while. I won't bite, I promise. Unless you want me to and I'll be more than happy to oblige!"

Logan's cheeks started to turn red as he couldn't help but blush at the fact that this beautiful chocolate sister was checking him out.

"I'm sorry, I didn't mean to embarrass you. I was just having fun with you. Loosen up, it's a party. So, how about you call your driver back and tell him to hold off on picking you up and I'll personally make sure you have a great time. So, in a sense, I'll be your bodyguard," Sariyah confirmed and laughed.

"Okay, so you're going to protect me?"

"Yes!" She replied with a smirk.

"Protect me from what? I don't see any danger," Logan stated, playing along with her.

"From all these women that are undressing you with their eyes!"

They both burst out laughing, and everyone turned to look at them trying to determine what was so funny. Logan's cheeks were warming up again.

"Come on. Have a look inside my office. I didn't want to do an office at first, but then I decided I needed a place for myself when I was tired, overworked, or just need to be alone," she informed him while grabbing his arm and leading him to her office.

Logan quickly texted his driver and told him to hold off on picking him up until he called again.

The office was painted a pink beige and had parquet flooring. Light Pink linen curtains hung over the one window in the office. The original lighting of the room had been replaced with a leaf-styled ceiling fan. There were candles everywhere, and she had two floor lamps, one in each corner of the room. Near the window, she had a small wooden coffee table with wicker basket drawer fronts and two basket weave chairs with white cushion and pink, beige, and brown pillows. She had a medium-sized pine desk on the other side of the room that was shaped like a table you may see in a kindergarten classroom where the teacher sits behind and about four students sit in front of her. The room was so relaxing, and the dimmed lights almost made the mood of the room, romantic, as if we were about to have a candlelight dinner.

"So, what do you think?" Sariyah asked interrupting Logan's thoughts.

"I like it. The atmosphere is so inviting, so relaxing, and so happy!" He replied as he sat in one of the wicker chairs near the window.

"Thanks! That's exactly what I was going for when I designed it," she boasted as she joined him by the window.

"Well, you did an awesome job! The place looks really nice. We probably should get back to your grand opening. We don't want people to think you are rude."

"They will be okay. This is my shop, remember? So, I set the rules. Do you mind if I take my shoes off for a minute? These heels are killing my feet!"

"As long as your feet don't stink, be my guest," he asserted with a chuckle.

She reached over and playfully hit him.

"I guess I do need to hire you to be my bodyguard, you don't play!" He declared sarcastically.

She took off her shoes and began rubbing her feet.

He couldn't help but notice her perfectly, pedicured toes, with a purple nail color that matched her chemise. All he could think was she has kissable feet.

"Do you mind if I do that for you?" He asked.

"Do what? Rub my feet?" she inquired skeptically.

"Yes! Rub your feet. I can see that you need a massage, and I would be less of a man to sit her and let you do it yourself."

Without waiting for her response, he got on the floor beside the wicker chair she sat in and began massaging her feet. The coffee table was in the way, so he pushed it to the side. Now he was directly in front of her massaging her feet.

Sariyah was melting on the inside at Logan's every touch. No man had ever given her a foot massage. EVER. The fact that a man she barely knew, a white man at that, was willing to rub her aching foot, was turning her on in the worse way. Call her crazy, but she was ready to give herself to him right then. She wasn't the one-night stand or sex on the first date type of girl, but her alter ego was knocking at the door, trying to get out. She squirmed in her seat, readjusting her legs and skirt, so her intimates wouldn't be visible to him as he massaged her feet.

Logan started massage from her feet to her calves and her thighs. The further up he went, the more she squirmed in her seat.

"Stop me anytime," he raved to her in his sexiest voice.

Looking down at him, she was mesmerized by his rich blue eyes. Her mind and heart were fighting. Her mind was telling her to get up and get out of there, but her body was telling her that she needed and wanted this. Her mind was losing the battle rather quickly as he moved further and further up her dress. She thought he was about to play in her honeypot, but he moved his hand to her stomach, under her shirt, and up to her curvaceous breasts that were almost spilling over her bra. No longer fighting her urge for some white chocolate, she pulled Logan face to hers and kissed him. Midway into the kiss she tried to pull away, but Logan pulled her deeper and deeper into him. She finally stopped resisting and went with the flow. After their tongues had played tug-of-war for what seemed like minutes, he started kissing on her cheeks and necks, stopping to suck on her earlobes and the dimples in her collarbone. He whispered in her ear how beautiful she was to him and planted small kisses on her ear back to her lips before he stopped and got up.

"You do feel as good as you look, but it would be so rude of us to continue to stay held up in your office. It is your grand opening, and you should be mingling with your customers and workers. I'll have my driver pick me up, and I'll call you in the morning," he volunteered.

15

"How are you going to call me and you don't have my number?" She contested.

"I don't have it yet, but you are about to give it to me," he gloated.

Sariyah just giggled and handed him her card. It took her a minute to regain her composure, but she knew he was right.

"You are right. You can wait for your driver in here if you want and I'll talk to you later. I need to rejoin the party and make my guests feel welcome," Sariyah stated while walking towards the door.

"Wait a minute," Logan replied, and he walked over to her and gave her another big kiss. "Enjoy your party, Miss James."

Before she did something she would regret, she hurriedly left the room and rejoined the party. Logan sat back down and called his driver. He didn't know what it was about Sariyah, but if there was such thing as love at first sight, he was coming down with a bad case of it.

He called his driver and waited inside her office. After a few minutes, he heard yelling and screaming. He tried to ignore the noise because it was none of his business, but the screams got louder and louder. Logan finally emerged from the office and found a guy pulling on Sariyah and all in her face yelling at her.

"Leave me alone, Craig. I told you that it was over! Get out of my shop!" She was screaming, but the guy wasn't bulging.

"I thought you weren't in there with nobody, Ri-Ri! There that motherfucker goes right there!" Craig specified pointing at Logan.

"He isn't my boyfriend; he is the mayor's son. He came here for the grand opening ceremony!" She screamed at Craig.

Craig let go of her shirt he was pulling on and started walking towards Logan. Logan didn't move but got into a defensive stance. Sariyah was yelling for Craig to leave

Logan alone, but Craig wouldn't listen. He approached Logan and started swearing and yelling in his face. What Craig didn't know was that Logan had a black belt in jiu-jitsu. Craig continued screaming in Logan's face.

"I don't know who you are, but you need to calm down and leave. Miss James, have already asked you to leave her place of business. If you don't leave, I will have to call the police," Logan voiced through clenched teeth.

He was trying so hard to be a gentleman, but he also didn't want to appear weak in Sariyah's eyes or have Craig think he was afraid of him.

"Call the motherfucking police! You go need 'em and the ambulance after I whoop your ass!" Craig threatened and raised his arm as if he was about to strike Logan.

Logan grabbed Craig's left arm with his right arm and swiftly swung him around. He inserted his left arm under Craig's left arm and reached around to the back of his head while his right hand held Craig's left arm to his chest and applied light pressure to Craig's neck and in less than ten seconds, Craig fell to the floor.

"Sariyah—Miss James, call the police," Logan stressed as he prepared to walk out the door. He texted his driver that he was ready to go.

"Wait, Logan," Sariyah said and followed him outside. "Thank you for what you did in there for me. Craig is an ex-boyfriend that has been stalking me for…"

"No offense, Miss James, but you don't owe me an explanation for his behavior. He should have never disrespected you or your place of business like that. You should get a restraining order against him because it's no telling what he is capable of."

"Okay, I will and thank you again for everything. I'm sorry the night ended so badly," Sariyah cited looking down.

Logan walked over to her and placed his finger under her chins and lifted up her head. "My night didn't end badly. I'm standing next to a beautiful, sexy, chocolate goddess. I'd say that's one heck of an ending."

His blue eyes capturing Sariyah's attention again and no longer able to hide the way he was making her feel, she reached up and kissed him. Logan kissed her back but pulled away as the police pulled in.

"I'll give you a call in the morning, to check on you; Logan declared before walking over to the officer to explain what happened. The officer then talked to Sariyah, just as Logan's driver pulled up.

"Officer, I'll be down in the morning to give my full statement. Good night, Miss James!" and he disappeared into the back seat of the black Lincoln Town car with the pitch black tint.

*****

The next morning, Logan awoke to his father beating on his door. He finally opened the door, avoiding eye contact with his father knowing what he wanted to talk about, and he immediately wished he hadn't answered it. His father was going on and on about the altercation at

Sariyah's shop then he starting talking about Logan's love for black women. As his father talked, Logan felt his body tensing and his heartbeat increase. His father was pissing him off. Logan drowned out most of the conversation until his father called Sariyah, *a black, ghetto, bitch.*

Logan was livid. His nostrils flared, and he started breathing noisily, and for the first time in his life, he was finally standing up to his father. He looked at his father with cold, hard, flinty eyes and said to him,

"Dad, you are wrong. Sariyah hasn't done anything to you. You don't even know her. You always want to tear down minorities as if they are less than you when the fact of the matter is our graves are going to be the same size. I don't even see how you go through life with so much hatred; it's tiring and lonely. I let you run Ashley away. I should have fought harder to protect her honor, but I didn't because I want to please my father and make him proud of me. The truth, I know you will never be proud of me, and I'm okay with that because I don't want your life.

I don't want to be the mayor of this corrupt town. Most of my life, I have been ashamed to be your son because of your racist attitude. Well, here's a reality check dad! Most of my closest friends are black. Some are Hispanics and other minorities. A few may even be gay or have a disability, but they are my friends, and you or anyone else can't tell me to stop being their friends. I love black women. I think they are some of the most beautiful women in the world. I have dated white girls, but I prefer dating black girls, and if things go well with Sariyah, she's going to be my woman and possibly my wife! So, I'm telling you now if you cannot accept any of that; then you can just leave my house right now!" Logan stated sternly.

His father winced at his words. He looked as if he wanted to say something to Logan but instead he just lowered his head and walked out of the house and slammed the door. Logan locked his door and went back to bed. He couldn't believe he had stood up to his father and he finally felt at peace. After years of cowering to his father's commands, he finally established his own.

*****

Sariyah laid awake all night with Logan McBride on her mind. She has never dated a white man before, but she was seriously smitten with Logan. The way everything played out yesterday left her feeling like she was in a modern-day Lifetime movie. She kept beating herself up for not getting his number. Now she was stuck waiting and wondering if he was going to call her.

Just as her mind was starting to accept the fact that she would probably never get another chance with Logan, her phone rang. She hurriedly answering her phone without looking at the number, she answered and prayed in her head that it was him.

"Good morning, beautiful! I hope you haven't eaten yet on this lovely, Saturday morning, because I want to treat you to breakfast, since our night together was so rudely interrupted," Logan declared.

Sariyah was so happy that he called her that she hoped up and immediately jumped up and down on the bed.

"Hello! Hello!" Logan cited into the phone.

"Oh, I'm sorry. I'm still waking up, but I would love to go to breakfast with you. I'm starving anyway, especially since I didn't eat much last night."

"Don't remind me about last night. I hated the night had to end. So, how bout you meet me at the mall. You can leave your car there and ride me to get breakfast."

"No! How about you tell me where you want to have breakfast, and I'll meet you," she insisted.

Not wanting to make her upset or cause her to cancel on him, Logan agreed.

"Meet me at the Crackel Barrel down from the mall in about thirty minutes. See you soon, beautiful."

"Okay," she stated and hung up to get dressed for her breakfast date with Logan.

*****

When Sariyah got to *Crackel Barrel*, Logan was waiting for her at the entrance. He was dressed down in

24

some black joggers and a white V-neck shirt with some black Nikes, but he still looked handsome as ever. They were twinning without even planning it; she had on black yoga pants, flip-flops, and a white *MUW* t-shirt.

"So, you trying to dress like me, huh?" he uttered to her.

"No, black and white is universal comfort clothes color, I guess!" she replied.

He simply laughed and held the door open for her to enter. After they were inside, he grabbed her hand and held it as they walked up to the hostess to be seated.

The hostess was a young, blond that looked as if she was still in high school or just starting college.

"How many?" She asked Logan while looking directly at him, refusing to acknowledge Sariyah that was standing right beside him and holding his hand.

Before Logan could answer, Sariyah asserted sternly, "Two!" That caught her attention and she quickly looked from Logan to Sariyah. Logan looked at Sariyah, his eyes telling her to *calm down and let him handle it* but her eyes were giving the waitress the message *not to fuck with her*, but either the waitress was bad at reading eyes and body languages or she didn't give a damn. After they were seated, she again looked at Logan and told him, "Your waitress will be here shortly", and walked off.

"It's okay, beautiful. I've dealt with plenty of ignorant people like that. Don't let her get too you. Plus, she's just mad that you snagged a sexy, piece of Vanilla!" Logan said while reaching across the table and grabbing Sariyah's hands.

She couldn't help but laugh. "Really? Is that what it is?"

"Yeah, look, she's still staring!" Logan muttered.

"Well, let's not be rude. Let's give her something to look at them. Sariyah got out of her chair and leaned over the table and kissed Logan. He kissed her back, and they kissed for what seemed like a minute or two. When they finally broke apart and looked up at the hostess stand, the hostess had disappeared. Logan and Sariyah burst out laughing.

"Well, my appetite just changed for something else. You wanna get out of here before she has her friends spit in our food or something?" Logan insisted.

"Sure, cause I would hate to catch a case and end up in a cell next to Craig for whooping her ass all over this restaurant."

Just as they were leaving, their waitress was approaching the table.

"We're leaving!" Logan stated and grabbed Sariyah's hands and walked out, with the waitress still standing there looking dumbfounded.

Standing against his car, she asked, "So where are we going to eat?"

Logan stood in front of her and asked, "Do you trust me, Sariyah?"

"Yeah, I guess I do. I feel comfortable around you, maybe too comfortable, because I still barely know you. So, how about we get something quick to eat and you can keep me company, while I clean up my shop. After you had left last night, everyone left, and I didn't get a chance to clean up. So, it will be like a do-over from last night without all the drama," she replied.

"Sure, I'd love that. I'll pick up us some breakfast from Jack's, and I'll meet you back at your shop. You're not allergic to anything that I should about, are you?" Logan inquired.

Sariyah laughed.

"Did I say something wrong?" He asked.

"No, you didn't. Most guys wouldn't ask about your allergies when they are offering to get you food; that's all."

"Well, I'm not most guys, and if you give me a chance, you are going to see that, I'm one of a kind, a rare breed!" he said and chuckled.

"Alright now, see you at the shop!" She said as she prepared to get in her car.

"Wait a minute," he commanded. He pulled her to him and kissed her with everything in him. She resisted a little, but after a few seconds gave into her desires for him. They kissed for minutes, before coming up for air.

"Be safe, beautiful."

Sariyah got into her car and pulled off. Watching her pull off, Logan knew two things. One, he was falling for Sariyah James and two, she was going to be MRS. LOGAN MCBRIDE!

Patti Doss is a Mississippi native. She is the CEO of Exquisite Reads Publications and Exquisite Literary Magazine. She is the author of the *Somebody Else's Husband* Series, *Finding Love at Christmas* (a Christmas novella), *A Woman's Love* (a poetry collection) and two children's books: *I Love to Write* (a Black History story) and *Never Too Busy* (a story about family love). She is also a blogger for *Urban Image Magazine* and a columnist for *Addictive Magazine*. She is also featured in Niyah Moore's Anthology, *Patron on Ice*, and will be featured in Xyla Turner's *Women Withstanding All* Anthology coming soon.

For more information about Patti Doss, please visit her website at authoresspattidoss.com or her company website at exquisitereadspublications.com.

For the Love of a woman

Anitra Hill

"When I saw you I fell in love, and you smiled because you knew."

-William Shakespeare

My father often warned me "Giani, these females are impossible to figure out. One thing that you must know is that females keep a lot of things to themselves. Like, you'll have her before she lets you know and you'll also lose her way before she tells you that it's over! So son if you're lucky enough to find a pot of gold, don't go chasing after any other rainbows!"

Giani Lynwood Gaveston Sr. was a very ingenious and smart man, it's a shame that he was too stubborn, bull headed and stuck on his pride to follow his own advice in the department of love. If he would listen to his own advice, which he has preached to me over the years, then just maybe he would have never lost his pot of gold!

31

Growing up as the Jr. of Giani Lynwood, I was constantly told how much I looked and acted just like him. My father was no stranger to the ladies; he was the true replica of the term "Ladies Man". He took pride in having a son who grew up to be just as charming as him as far as the ladies were concerned. He made sure that I was groomed and raised to love the female specimen with all of me. I had that part mastered and that was definitely considered a gift and a curse. A gift because I had a way of making women smile and feel better about themselves. Now, the cursed part about it is that because of my gift it made it hard for me to hold onto a relationship.

Nowadays, people are addicted to a lot of different things. Some have a weed and alcohol addiction while some others were recreational drugs. Also, people had shopping addictions but my Guilty Addiction was different from all of those. I'm 30-year-old, Giani Gaveston Jr. and I have a Guilty Addiction to the ladies! I love the female specimen; I worship and cherish everything about them. A woman that's loved properly is what you can call a real live Superwoman. God's greatest creation of the world is the woman and I love them just as such. If you make and keep a woman happy, then she will move mountains for you, and do anything in her power to keep "hers" happy. When God created the woman, he was truly showing off. They come in all shapes, sizes, and colors and I love them all. It is sure to be something about each and every female that makes her unique and so easy to love. Just because I tell you that my addiction is the ladies that doesn't mean that I'm having sex with all of the ladies. Let me tell you a little about My Guilty Addiction!!

Chapter 1: Getting to know Giani

I was born and raised for the first 10 years of my life in North Philly. Philly taught me so much about the street life at such an early age. My parents tried to shelter me from the street part of life, but to their surprise, I already had most of the streets down packed due to my Uncle Red. While they were working Uncle Red looked after me and I hung with him in the mean streets of Philadelphia. The City of Brotherly Love showed me the ropes and prepared me for anything that this rough and cold world could offer. I've seen people get shot, stabbed, women get raped and kids become victims of the streets way too early. Drugs, guns, and crime, were the most common things that people thought of when they thought of Philly.

When I turned 10, my father's luck with the ladies ran out. He and my mother had a great life together, so I thought. My Pops loved the ladies and my mother suffered from this one fact. He gave my mother the world. When I say the world that included heartache, pain and a whole lot of side women to go along with it. The difference between my father and I was that I wouldn't commit to a woman because my goal was to never hurt them, just to make them smile. So, I promised myself that I would wait until I was ready. But my dad, on the other hand, didn't know how to leave his affairs in the streets or to leave his addiction alone and be a one woman man. He was married for 17 years to my mother but had numerous affairs on her. Her appearance had changed over the years; she started to look older in her face from worrying about the issues that he brought to her. She was a real life beauty queen in my eyes and Pops was lucky to have her. Many men hoped and wished for a woman like my mother. She was a hard working wife and mother and held her RN nursing job down for over 21 years. She was a natural born people person and a real nurturer. That was her gift and also her curse as well, simply because it was in her heart to take care of others. However, often times when she was supposed to walk away, she stayed and neglected to turn her back on others even when it was time to. My mother Jewel Gaveston was my life and it hurt me to see her hurting like she was. I loved my father as well, but it was clear that he didn't deserve my mother. My mother was too good for him, and I refused to ruin a woman like my father did my mother. She no longer believed in herself or in true love. I wanted to make women like my mother believe again, just to see them smile.

On my mother's 40th birthday, my pops gave her the worst birthday gift ever. Unlike, the previous years where she was to get a brand new car or a new diamond ring for her celebration of another year of life, this year she received a paternity test from some female named Julia James. This small weight piece of paper contained the heavy weight information that Giani Gaveston Sr was 99.99% the father of 6-month-old Gracie LeAnne James. This petite framed lady had the nerve to knock on our door with this beautiful little girl with the prettiest smile ever in her arms. I heard the doorbell ring and my mother and I both went for the door at the same time. She opened it as I stood there to see who was there standing to greet us. As soon as my momma answered the door the lady's tears began to flow uncontrollably, her legs got weak and my mother had an uncertain but certain look on her face when she looked into the eyes of the broken female that stood helplessly before her. The baby girl looked at me in the eyes and gave me the biggest and, prettiest grin that I had ever seen. As my mother held the lady up for comfort. I took the little princess in my arms not even aware that she was my kin.

My mother invited the helpless lady into our home without even having confirmation of who she really was. The room fell silent for what seemed like 20 minutes. The only sounds that you heard were the ticking of the wall length grandfather clock on our wall in the foyer. Also, the coos of the beautiful yet innocent baby girl that sat in my arms as if she knew that I was her big brother that would be her protector for life. The broken woman finally spoke and her words seemed to cave in every wall inside of our home.

"Jewel, my name is Julia and I'm just finding out that I have given birth to my beautiful princess Gracie and your husband is the father". She sniffled again and removed a piece of paper from her handbag and handed it to my mother and assured her that she knew nothing of her or their marriage. My father had been living a double life and slipped up and fathered another life besides me. My mother cried and cried as the 2 of the ladies comforted one another. Gracie LeAnne laid her head on my chest as she watched our mothers cry tears of hurt and this made me a stronger man. I had to be the man to my mother, this lady and also my baby sister that my father wasn't here to be. At 10 years old, I felt as if I was more of a man than my Pops had ever been at that very moment. I held all 3 ladies and from that point on I knew that it was my purpose on earth to comfort and to ease the pain of women. From that moment on I made it my goal to put a smile on each woman that I came in contact with and grew to have a passion for the feelings of women.

On that day, my mother's birthday, my mom exchanged contact information with the lady who had mothered my little sister. They promised to make sure that we would stay in each other's life. My mother saw the love that I had in my eye's for my little sister and never wanted to take that opportunity from me to grow up in her life. After about 2 hours of them talking and Julia takes pictures of my sister and I she stood up to leave and told my mother that she was sorry for barging in and giving her such bad news on her special day but she told her that she was glad to have connected with 2 beautiful people. She turned to me and said, "Thank you Giani for loving my daughter for the innocent angel that she is and please promise me that whatever is to happen that you will always love and protect her for me". I looked at this broken hearted soul and wished that I could fix her, but I gave her my word. I meant that I would love this little person with everything in me! They left and my mother decided to pack up our clothes and we left the State of Philadelphia without even letting my father know or even saying goodbye.

Chapter 2: 20 years later

20 years later, my mother and I now reside in Richmond, Virginia and doing better than ever. My mother is still in the nursing field doing what she loved to do and is happier than I have ever seen her. I'm now a 30-year-old grown man with no kids. I am, still loving and watching over my baby sister like I promised Ms. James. Gracie is now 20 years old. Following in my footsteps, she is now a college student at VCU here in Richmond, Virginia as I was. Her mother had passed away about 15 years ago from cervical cancer. Before she left this earth, she asked my mother if she would look after Gracie and my mother agreed. My mother had fallen in love with Gracie just as I had a long time ago. So before Julia had gone on to be with

the Lord, she made sure that Gracie was comfortable and settled in with us and did the proper paperwork to make everything legal with the courts. Gracie loved being there with my mom and me. She was a great child that looked up to me. I made sure that she stayed focused with her schooling and she ended up being an honor roll student all through her school years.

My schooling has paid off, which has made my mother proud of my accomplishments. I'm a high school guidance counselor. Every day dealing with these kids makes my job worth doing. Making a difference in someone's life always has made me feel complete. I put so much into my career and my family that it doesn't bother me to still be single. I have females that I entertain and make it my business to keep happy, but I vowed to myself that I would not get into anything that I couldn't commit to. I refused to hurt another female like I had to watch my father do. My mother still refuses to date because of what he has put her through. She doesn't even take men seriously anymore. My father is now paying for everything that he has put my mother and all of those other women through. He has not been the same since my mom and I up and left him. He has tried for years to get her back, but she has shown her inner strength by keeping her promise of not going back. He's had bad luck and ill health ever since he lost his pot of gold. My sister doesn't even know our father and she is probably best off like that because he doesn't know how to love her or any other woman properly. I still deal with him, but not like I want to because my loyalty is with my mother. He damaged her so I can't possibly respect him as I once did before I knew better. I don't disrespect him, but I had less respect for him before I knew what it was to love a woman so much to make her a better woman. Even at 30 years old, I still take my mother out on dates, send her roses and gifts just to see her smile. I have made it my lifelong goal to make sure that my mother and my sister never have to look for love or validation from any other man. I will show them how they deserve to be treated even when any other man does not.

Chapter 3: The starters on my All-Star Team

The closest thing that I ever had to a girlfriend was my longtime high school friend Passion Rogers. She deserved the world on a silver platter, but I just couldn't give it to her. Don't get me wrong, I treated her like the Princess that she was but I just was scared to fully commit to her because I didn't want to ever hurt her. I did everything that a great boyfriend would do if I were a boyfriend. I took her out on dates and made sure that I was there whenever she needed me, she understood me almost better than anyone besides my mother and sister. She was the next best thing to perfect, she didn't pressure me because she knew that she had a big portion of my heart. I had several female friends, but none of them came before Passion. There were many guys that tried to get with her but she didn't want anyone but me. I knew and understood our bond, but I think that I took her heart for granted by thinking that she would always wait for me to be ready to settle down. I always thought that Passion would be my wife, but then again maybe not. After Passion had gone off to school in North Carolina we began to speak less and less, I went and saw her a few times while she was in school but then our time together became far and few in between. She then stopped answering my calls. After that, I met Gina from Atlanta. When we began to start chilling more and more, I stopped bothering to even get in contact with Passion. She would contact me when she felt that she was ready to. I have to admit though it hurt like hell and Gina was just someone to pass the time. She was a very gorgeous and cool girl, but she was no Passion.

For Gracie's 21st birthday, she wanted to go party in DC. So, 3 of her homegirls and me took a road trip to DC to party. They were all getting lit on the car ride and at the hotel. While I made sure that they were good, I only slightly sipped on the liquid substance that made my eyes a little chink. But I was ready to make sure that my little sister bought in her 21st birthday how she wanted it. It meant everything to me that she even wanted to bring it in with me. Her best friend Sade had a thing for me, but Gracie didn't play that about her big brother and I tried to respect that. To my surprise, the ladies wanted to go to the strip club called Shakers. It was a Co-ed strip club where there were male and female dancers. This was the livest strip club besides the Atlanta and Miami strip club scene. Leaving the 5-star upscale hotel was when Sade tried to throw herself on me, I loved my women and also loved pussy but I respected her as my sister's best friend. I knew that I would turn her out and I didn't want to do that to her. Being around Sade made me realize how she moved. She fell hard for the guys that she dealt with so I refused to take her goods from her. Sade was fine as hell, but I had to think with my big head and not my small head. My father would have taken those buns and not thought twice about it.

Pulling up at the brightly lit strip club made me think that this wasn't such a good idea. I didn't know if I was ready to see my little sister live in action, but then I had to realize that she was now grown. I had to let her become the grown woman that she now was and trust her judgment. As soon as we stepped into the club we were escorted to our V.I.P section and the bottles started coming our way as I had previously set up. Gracie came over and hugged me and told me that she was glad that God had blessed her with the best brother ever and I was her very best friend. She then whispered "Thank you for staying loyal, and not fucking Sade. I know that bitch threw herself at you bro and you curved her. You thought that I didn't know what it was, didn't you?" She then gave me a high five and called a brown skinned shorty over to our section and told her "Give my brother a lap dance honey and call a friend". She

46

turned it into our birthday, we had so much fun. We both tipped the dancers well. That's when the unimaginable happened, in walked Passion Rogers. The body was banging and she was no longer my high school sweetheart or my best friend; she was now known as Vixen. Everything was exposed, she was no longer my innocent Pash, and she was now everybody's desire. Rage and confusion had rushed through me and I didn't know why. It was no longer my business what she did with her life. She chose not to deal with me anymore and now I see why. Instead of staying there to enjoy the females before me, I walked off and looked her dead in the eyes and she looked as if she was embarrassed for me to see her like that. She called my name but I kept going, I had to get out of her presence before I became disrespectful. I had never disrespected Passion before and I wanted to leave it like that.

Entering the men's room, I had a flashback of her flawless body and the anger turned into desire and at that moment, I thought back to the time that I had taken her virginity. That was the very first time that she had ever let anyone see her in a sexual sight and I thought that it would always be that way but to my surprise I was wrong. I began to stroke my manhood right there inside of the stall at the thought of her tight wet pussy sitting on my dick, then came the rage again. My thoughts were interrupted by the sound of someone coming inside of the bathroom. I quickly snapped out of it and put my erect crooked dick back inside of my designer jeans. As I began to exit the stall, it was her right there in the flesh. Passion "Vixen" Rogers, wasn't as beautiful as she was before, she looked as if life has thrown her a couple of curve balls and she was losing the game. Her body was flawless, but her eyes, which used to be my favorite part of her face now was filled with sadness. She had an untold story about her and I needed to know her deal. "What has happened to my baby?" I asked, looking into her saddened eyes. A single tear fell from her slanted eyes as she grabbed my neck and sobbed. Her innocence was right in front this new person that I had seen a few minutes earlier and me.

In between cries she said, "They raped me Giani, they stripped me of my dignity". "Who raped you Pash, who did this to you? "She looked at me in shame and just cried, it was as if she was ashamed to tell me. I didn't pressure her to tell me anything, I allowed her to get it all out. She would talk to me when she was ready. Leaving out of the bathroom we went into a private room at the back of the club and that's when she broke it all down to me. When she was in school, some guy named Chill that she had been messing with allowed his homeboys to rape her simply because he was jealous of me. He felt as if she was acting like a whore for still dealing with me then he would treat her like a whore. He and 3 of his friends took all of her dignity from her so she dropped out of school and never had any more communication with any of her old friends. She felt ashamed and alone in this world. She was upset with me at that point in her life because I wasn't there to protect her, she said that I was busy being a good man to everyone else that I forgot about her and had started to put others before her. She started to cry again and said "Giani, I put my life on hold for you and I just wanted to be the woman that you chose but I just wasn't good enough for you. You're the only man that I have ever loved besides my daughter's father. Yes, I have a daughter now and I named her after you Giani because you showed me how real love was supposed to feel. I want my daughter to know how real love feels. I thank you for being who you have been to me in my past and for showing me what love felt like, you just didn't want what I wanted at that time. I know that you loved me Giani but that wasn't enough to hold us together". I hadn't realized that while I was busy trying not to destroy her by hurting her, I had failed her and hurt her anyways. It felt as if I had stabbed myself in the heart, I never intended for things going like this and I never wanted to see Passion feel an ounce of hurt but I did. "I'm no better than my father", I said as I looked deep into her damaged soul. I'm sorry Passion, I'm sorry for not loving you as you deserved to be loved. I'm sorry for what those cowards stripped of you. I'm so sorry baby, I wanted you to be my wife. I just didn't want to hurt you before I was ready to step to you. She hugged me so tight that let me know that she forgave me. However, I can't honestly say that I forgive myself. We talked for another 15 minutes and then we exchanged numbers and she said that she wanted me to meet my goddaughter that I didn't know that I had and her father. I agreed and realized that I now had my best friend back and I was satisfied with that. Leaving out of the private room with Passion I felt relieved to know that after all that has happened in her life that she has finally found her happiness in her daughter little miss Giani.

Entering back into the V.I.P section where I found Gracie and her friends enjoying themselves with a few male and female strippers, I now felt more whole than before. Gracie came over and hugged me so tight and told me how much she thanked God for her mother coming to my mother's house and telling our mother about our no good ass father. This made my heart melt because Gracie didn't talk about the past much. She held in a lot of hurt and pain from losing her mother and then that she didn't have a father that she felt cared about her. Inside I kind of hate my father for the hurt that he caused the females in my life and also for my guilty addiction to these women. Even though I thought that I had mastered the art of making these beautiful creatures on earth happy, I still managed to hurt one of the women that meant the most to me.

Just as I had given up on finding a love of my own was when my baby sister had become pregnant with her very first child who was a little boy. My very own nephew, I promised to teach him the right way to love a woman and to have an unconditional love for his mother. My sister is the happiest that she has been in a very long time, it was as if she wanted so much more out of life. My mother was happy as well to become a grandmother, she said that it seemed as if I would never give her any grandkids so my sister was just as good.

On an early Saturday morning, I was awakened by my mother calling to tell my sister and me that my father and Uncle Red had just been murdered in Philly. We all headed out to Philly to be there for our Philly family and to see exactly what was going on. Pulling up to our old house brought back so many memories, including the very first time that I had laid eyes on my baby sister with the killer smile that stole my heart. Hearing the story from my grandmother on my Pop's side of how 2 guys pulled up on my father and my uncle at the store and blew both of their brains out in broad daylight in front of the ABC store. Rumors were that it was behind a female, but no one knows for sure. Looking at my father lying there made us realize that my sister and I looked exactly like our Pops, my mother's heart was broken. After all, of these years, my mom had finally admitted that she still loved my pops and she once had hopes of them making things right. She was saving herself for him to get himself together. She had her heart on reserve and now he was taken from her for good. She hugged us tightly and we watched as her heart continued to break into pieces.

Six weeks after we buried our father and uncle it was time to bury our very own mother. Jewel Gaveston died of a broken heart and she no longer wanted to be here on earth without her Giani Sr. The death of our mother, saddened us both, but we somehow found peace in knowing that she was now with the love of her life. It was very hard to lose both of our parents so close apart, but prayer and the love for one another made us realize that they have to be strong for each other and that God makes no mistakes.

On our mother's birthday was the day that changed both of our lives forever. Gracie went into labor and her son's father, Chuck called me to tell me that they were on their way to Richmond General Hospital. I was at work in a meeting, but that didn't stop me from leaving work at that very moment to join my only sister and brother in law for the happiest day of their life. By the time I made it to the delivery room there, she was the most beautiful woman that I had ever laid eyes on besides my mother. Matter of fact, she reminded me of my mother, she was Gracie's nurse Milani. Milani was breathtaking, she cared for my sister as if she was her own sister. She had a glow about her, and then as I looked her over and realized that the glow came from her bulging little belly that sat in front of her. She looked to be about 4 months pregnant and that broke my heart until Gracie says "Milani I think that someone has the hots for you" and then nods at me. I must have made it obvious that I was blinded by her beauty because she smiled and then told Gracie "Ahhhh he doesn't want my old pregnant behind, ever since I came with a package no one looks at me anymore" she laughed and then continued to get Gracie ready for her delivery. She was just so graceful and classy and I wish that I could have met her before she had gotten knocked up because I would have surely tried my hand in scooping her up.

Gracie started to fuss Chuck out and telling him to get out of her room and that she didn't want him there. Come to find out she was fussing because Chuck didn't have the baby's diaper bag, but she must have forgotten that she gave the diaper bag to me because she knew that I wouldn't forget it. "Calm down Gracie, I have the bag. Its right here, you gave it to me 2 weeks ago. Leave my bro in law alone he has done nothing wrong. At that time Gracie was hit with another contraction and Milani told Gracie "Girl, you're lucky to have a child's father that cares, my baby don't have a father. I'm in this alone so count your blessings my dear". Gracie looked at Milani and told her "I'm sorry sis, you're right". At that time, there was a big contraction and about 7 pushes later came a 7 pound 8-ounce baby boy named Cianni (See-Ahn-Nee) James. It was a beautiful sight and it was one that I'm lucky to have experienced.

I stepped outside of the hospital room to give the nurses a chance to clean the baby up and to also get my sister right. I was happy to leave because I needed to take a mental break. Things were starting to get the best of me because I was wishing that my mother was there to witness her grandson being born. Watching Milani in action reminded me of my mother at work, she was an RN just as my mother was and they also favored. Milani walked

outside of the room and asked me if I was ok. That's when
I felt as if I had to shoot my shot, so I asked her if I could
take her out and get to know her better and she agreed after
hesitating. Gracie had already given her the 411 on me and
so she already knew that she was going to give me a
chance. Thankfully, I had tried to shoot my shot because
just as my father once told me "Son, you'll have her way
before she lets you know, and you'll lose her way before
she says that it's over". I looked up at the ceiling and
smiled because I knew that my father was proud and my
mother would be satisfied as well.

Milani went to clock out after she finished up with my
sister and she came back into her room and sat with us and
we all enjoyed one another's company. Milani told us her
story and how she ended up being left alone to raise her son
by herself. Her daughter's father was killed by a stray
bullet coming from work. There was a shootout at the
convenience store that he had stopped at to get some gas

from and one of the bullets hit him in the temple and killed him instantly, and that left her to go through her pregnancy alone. Milani London was a great woman and she was put in an unfortunate situation, but it is something about her that makes me want to be there for her and make her life and the life of her unborn a beautiful one.

After about 2 months of us being inseparable, Milani was beginning to believe in love once again as she should because I feel as if God had handpicked her just for me and me for her. I treated her like the queen that she was and made sure that she wanted for nothing. I asked her if she minded if I attended her doctor's appointments with her and she agreed. From that point on when I heard Baby Journey's heartbeat I was in love with two women once again. Milani and Journey were now my main focus outside of my sister and my nephew. There was my mother in my ear telling me that she loved her new daughter in law and granddaughter and this made me know that I was making the right decision. After her 6-month doctor's appointment, I had planned a surprise dinner with Gracie and Chuck and that was where I got down on my knee and asked her to be my wife and also if I could adopt Journey. She agreed and from that day forward I never chased another rainbow but only found new ways to make my pot of gold the happiest in life!!!

What once was my guilty addiction has now turned into My Love For a Woman. That woman is my wife Milani London Gaveston and my princess Journey Jewel Gaveston!!!!

Anitra Hill is from Hampton, Virginia. She is a professional Customer Service Coordinator and also a published author. She started writing at a very young age. Writing is her passion and also her therapy. She is an Urban fiction author that is looking to spread my wings and explore off into different genres!

Her current published titles include: *The Right One Wrong Time, The Right One Wrong Time 2, And The Game Chose Me.* Her upcoming projects include *The Right One Wrong Time 3, Carter's Little Secret and Also Love Slave.* There will be many more great novels to come! For more information about Anitra, you can find her on Facebook: Author Anitra Hill Hill or IG: MRS_TALK_OF_THE_TOWN

Ring of Fire

Niyah Moore

"It is not in the stars to hold our destiny, but in ourselves."

-William Shakespeare

ROUND 1

It was a Friday night and after a long day at work, Kaori and two of her friends couldn't wait to unwind at Raglan, a small Irish Pub they always went to in their neighborhood. They drank Kilkenny Irish Cream Ales and ate Philly Cheese Steak Sandwiches and fries at a high pub table in the middle of the room.

Stephanie said to Kaori, "Two long years of nothing by booty-calling and you aren't bored yet? You have to be tired of this life by now."

Kaori threw her head back and laughed. "I don't have time for that bullshit."

"You're a cold piece of work," Vivica said. "If I were a man, I wouldn't even fool with you."

"I'm single," Kaori reminded them, "And, you're both married, so of course, you wouldn't understand."

"But, isn't Taariq trying everything to get you into a relationship?"

"Relationships are against my rules, Vivica. You know that."

"You don't let anyone get too deep with you, Kaori, regardless! It's like your coochie is on a time-out from falling in love."

Vivica laughed.

"What are you afraid of, girl?" Stephanie asked as she sipped her beer.

"I'm not afraid of anything," Kaori lied. "I just haven't met the right one. When I meet the right one, then just maybe I'll put my g-string on ice."

Vivica put down her glass and gave her best friend the side-eye. "I don't think you know how to put them hot things on ice."

"The damn ice would melt," Stephanie spat.

They laughed some more.

While they cracked up, Kaori noticed a caramelized brother with a five o'clock shadow beard sitting in the corner talking and having dinner with a group of men. His laughter with his friends had caught her attention all the way from across the room. His medium brown eyes drifted to where Kaori was sitting. It was at that very moment that she had turned her head in mid-laugh, and their eyes met. He was dressed in a signature black bomber leather jacket, white shirt underneath, and dark blue 501 jeans. She couldn't see his shoes, but she licked her lips and couldn't focus on what her girls were talking about now.

"Hello, Earth to Kaori. Girl, who just made you stop all conversation?" Stephanie asked, moving her head in the direction in which Kaori was gawking.

"I have to pee," Kaori said all of a sudden, scooting back from the table.

Though beer always ran through her too quickly, she knew she was going across the pub to do more than just relieve her bladder. She had to pass his table to get to the bathroom, and she was going to use that to see him up close. No thoughts of being nervous were present until she was near him. The first glimpse of his sparkling eyes meeting hers at this close distance, not only made her heart skip a few beats, it threatened to stop altogether. Saying that man was fine was an understatement. He was the epitome of what her ideal man looked like down to the scars and presumably tattoos.

The way he didn't blink while she approached and the way he dared her to stare back had her intrigued even more. His eyes watched her until she disappeared into the bathroom. *The Law of Attraction* left her to fantasize the unknown with a man she didn't even know.

While Kaori emptied her bladder, washed her hands, dried them, and then fixed her long hair to make sure she looked just as good as she did when she left the house.

Kaori fussed over her hair and would've touched up her lip gloss, only if it wasn't at the table in her purse.

After taking a deep breath, she walked briskly until she reached his table, where he seemed to be waiting for her. Instead of passing him up completely, she took a chance and stopped. Her nerves confirmed that she was standing in front of him because they were jumping.

She thought quickly on her feet and asked smoothly, "Don't I know you?"

He replied with a serious expression, "I don't think so."

She thought she felt the heaven's gates open up just for her because the sound of his baritone was heavenly.

"Are you sure? I feel like I know you from somewhere."

"I'm positive. I never forget a face."

Feeling her nerves get the best of her, she suddenly felt silly for even making up something so crazy when she never seen this man in her life. Now, his friends were looking at her.

"I'm sorry." She tried to walk away, but he stood up to stop her.

"Wait… Maybe you do look familiar."

Standing at six feet and five inches of pure sexiness, she stared up into his eyes and her heart plummeted into her stomach and started beating there.

"No, I thought you were someone else I knew. I'm sorry. Have a nice night."

He blocked her path a little bit, not invading, but subtly. "Wait a minute. Since there's been a clear mistake of identity… My name is Quadim. What's yours?"

Finding her voice that wanted to run away from her, she replied, "My name is Kaori."

He extended his hand to her. "It's very nice to meet you."

"It's nice to meet you as well." Shaking his hand, she could feel the chemistry coming from his palm, so she casually let go.

"Can I call you sometime?"

She twisted her lips into a smile. "How about I call you?"

"A man is always supposed to check in with a woman to see if she needs anything, not the other way around. So, how about I call you?"

Astonished, Kaori could only imagine how the color filling her cheeks had betrayed her attempt to seem reserved. There was no secret that the attraction was tangible. Kaori knew, by the way, he didn't smile and held her gaze that she wouldn't be able to collect his number like her other conquests. If she wanted him, which she did, she would have to fight this bout another way, *his* way.

Quadim pulled out his phone and handed it to her. She timidly punched in her number and saved her under his contacts. As she handed it to him, his hand covered hers. The phone didn't matter. The way to her did.

Slick bastard, she thought to herself as she smiled knowingly. "Call me after seven tomorrow."

"I will," he smirked softly. "Have a lovely evening, Kaori."

She sauntered away but peered back at him with a smile only to finally see a dazzling smile given in return.

As he watched her join her friends, he signaled the waiter before making his assumptions about her.

"That's what you call fine," Tab said to Quadim.

"That kind of shit never happens to me," Jamar added.

"Hey, if she hadn't stopped, I would've followed her back to her table anyway. I saw her when she first walked in and joined her friends."

Kaori couldn't help but smile because he was still staring at her. She dropped her eyes bashfully.

"Are you going to call him, girl?" Stephanie asked.

"I would, but I didn't get his number... I gave him mine..."

Stephanie and Vivica stared at each other before resetting their dumbfounded gazes back on her. Kaori *never* gave out her number first.

"You're going to pick up when he calls, right?" Stephanie asked. "You're not going to play that phone-tag crap that you do, are you?"

"I don't know. It's like I can see it in his eyes. He would make me fall in love with him."

Vivica gasped while Stephanie gave Kaori a wide-eyed look.

"Why you two looking at me like that?"

"Because if that man can make you fall in love, then he would accomplish the impossible," Vivica said.

"The impossible? You're too funny," Kaori laughed.

"It's not like you fall in love easily. Kaori, you avoid love like it's the black plague. I wouldn't be surprised if he ended up being just another number in your cell phone. That's if he even makes it that far."

Kaori thought of what her friends were saying. They weren't lying, and the drumming of her heart confirmed that it would be best to ignore him when and if he called.

***

ROUND 2

Kaori was in his bedroom, lying on his bed. The way she looked at him made him want to be the only one she ever looked at that way again. The smell of her was intoxicating as she lay underneath him. Her soft breath darted in and out as her chest rose and fell in a heightened fashion. Kaori bit her bottom lip as she gazed up at him. Quadim had contemplated this moment for months as they got to know one another over the phone. Now, he had managed to get her to come over. Talking on the phone was good because they fell for one another hard, but there was nothing like talking in person.

Quadim had wanted to walk up to her when she first walked into the pub and sweep her off her feet. Something about her made him want to risk everything for the moment and take the opportunity to discover what beautiful felt like without even knowing her name, yet, he didn't even approach her. He *felt* so attracted to her lighter shade of browned skin, Asian slanted eyes, and long jet-black hair. He learned her favorite color was turquoise, and she appreciated flowers but loved Tulips. She was mixed; her mother was Japanese, and her father was Black. She was twenty-five and didn't have any children, and she was a customer service representative for an insurance company.

Kaori fought with whether or not she should've answered his calls at first. After careful consideration, she decided to explore her new option. She only expected dinner on their first date. *How did she end up going to his house afterward?*

In the back of her mind, immediate thoughts of leaving came to mind, but there was something about his honesty that made her trust him. He didn't have children, but he had been divorced for four years. He designed furniture for a huge corporation, and his loft was impeccable. He was like no other man she had ever met in her life.

Maybe it was simply his imagination, but he felt as if he loved her already. She was underneath him, fully dressed, and this night had almost seemed as if it would never happen. He didn't think that offering her some wine at his place after dinner would hold her attention, but she accepted without hesitation to his surprise.

Her beauty clouded his mind unlike any of the other women he had dated and kicked to the curb afterward. As he stared down into her eyes, he realized there was nothing to be nervous about. Regardless of what was going to happen, he was ready for whatever the outcome would be. He made her laugh at dinner, and now he bent down to taste the wine that soaked her thick lips without even asking.

"You're not allowed to kiss me that way," she said with a serious expression.

Ignoring her, Quadim kissed Kaori again anyway. With both of their eyes closed, his lips covered hers, and as he sucked on her bottom lip, his tongue ran across it slowly.

Moaning, too loudly, she bit his bottom lip hard in a playful manner.

"Ouch," he said with a slight frown.

She giggled. "I told you that you weren't allowed to do that."

"I can't kiss you now?" he asked, staring deeply into her eyes.

"Don't you want to try again?"

"Oh, so you want me to chase you," he smirked. "I won't chase you. I don't have to. You're lying right here under me."

Kaori uttered, slow and coolly, "C'mere."

"Only if you promise not to bite me again…"

"C'mere."

He kissed her again, and she didn't bite him. Nothing was on either one of their minds except the way the other felt. Desire and fire had set their action aflame, as their sense of longing became excited by the pure enjoyment of one another.

He pulled her roughly to him and sucked her lips, not giving her the opportunity to bite him again. She sucked his tongue, matching his intensity. A soft moan escaped her while his passion was one that she had never experienced. His kisses and tongue moved down to her chin, neck, and décolleté.

"What you want to do next?" she asked, breathing heavily.

Quadim envisioned them driving down to the water and walking along the beach, but the look on her face was too cute, and he didn't want to interrupt this moment. Mesmerized by the smoky eye shadow that blended into the neutral browns that highlighted her eyes, Quadim whispered, "Let's just go with the flow."

She whispered back, "How do you want to do this?"

He observed her hint of arousal. "Let me show you."

Quadim slid his hands to the sides of her dress and squeezed her waist before he picked her up from the bed. While she giggled infectiously, he spoke as he lifted her higher, "I'm going to do this *my* way."

Quadim walked Kaori towards the wall, pressed her there while he bent down, and spread her legs apart to remove her panties. Kaori lifted her dress up by the fistfuls until it was gathered above her waist. With her dress up and her lust exposed, Quadim positioned her legs on his shoulders and left his kiss on her second set of lips. Soft licks were given. His moans sent vibrations through her that made her lose her new fear of falling for anyone.

Each of her lips was sucked slowly and pulled softly into his mouth, as he held them in place with his tongue. Quadim ate her just like how he kissed, intensely. His tongue worked into the motions seamlessly, and before he could get into his rhythm, Kaori was screaming, "Put me down!"

She hated to come so quick because it made her feel powerless, weak, defeated, and she hated that. Anytime she let a man hold that kind of power over her; she always ended up feeling indignant. She felt violated that he could have such jurisdiction over her body, and the fear she felt in the power of the orgasm that was on the rise was like a wave drawn unseen out to sea.

She had another thing coming, though, because there was no way he was going to put her down at *her* command. This was his time to show her just how much dominance he had with his tongue, alone.

Her voice died in her throat as she held her breath and exhaled, "No…"

He whispered against her clit, "Yes."

As he took her from that wall to the other, Kaori gripped his head tightly, clenching as she exploded rainbows and saw only colors behind her close eyelids due to the rush of pleasure.

"...Quadim." Her guttural burst found the air and echoed off his bedroom walls.

He walked with her through his conversation with her lovely kitty never ceased or interrupted, he slowly brought her parallel to the floor. Kaori found herself bucking towards the ceiling until her screams hit a high pitch and she shook. As her twitching slowed, he used his hands to remove the only things that were separating them— their clothes. Lying on his soft carpet, their nakedness felt right. Suddenly, he stopped. Kaori opened her eyes with a puzzled look.

"What's the matter?" she asked as her hands went to his face.

He rolled onto his back with her in his arms, placing her on top of him. His hardness was begging to be used, but instead, he ran his fingers over her ear and pushed the hair back from her face. She stared at him briefly before the heat caught her face and she felt herself blush. No one had *ever* looked at her like that.

"Why are you staring at me like that?" she thought aloud.

"Because I can."

His way with her was unbelievable. A match he had been from the start and her trepidation was replaced with a thrilling sensation throughout her whole body. Kaori leaned down and kissed the side of Quadim's neck before she ran her hand down his side, over his hip, down his thigh, and over to his center. Lowering her kisses along his body, she tongue massaged him, over to the very tip of his hardened flesh until he was nice and wet. Once she had him all the way in her mouth, he groaned and clutched her hair with both hands. As her mouth formed an "O", her tongue slivered along the sides of him. Her eyes couldn't help but close as soon as he thrust up towards her.

"Damn," he exasperated breathlessly as he pulled her up and laid her on her back.

He entered her. The look in his eyes wasn't the only thing that told her he was falling for her. She could feel him with every stroke. He placed her legs on his shoulder and stirred inside the very deepest of her deep.

Once they were done, she rested in his arms. She rubbed his chest while his hands were in her hair that had been dampened by her sweat. Felt *too good*. Suddenly, envious thoughts of all the possible types of women who lay underneath him bombarded her. *How many beautiful women had he been with? Did that even matter?* She closed her eyes tightly and hoped she wasn't making a mistake by letting him get this close to her.

"I can't believe this," Kaori said as she played with the hairs on his chest with her fingertips.

"What can't you believe?"

She rested on her elbow and stared into his deep eyes. "I'm here with you… and I haven't left yet. Usually, by now, I would've had my clothes already back on."

He hummed while rubbing her back, "Well, I'm glad you're still here… Kiss me, beautiful."

***

ROUND 3

Kaori lifted her head from his down pillow as soon as the first ray of sunlight beamed on her face. Judging by the way that Quadim was sleeping soundless, she hadn't interrupted him at all. Smiling, she recollected the whole evening in its entirety like a lightning bolt flashing before her eyes and felt her heart sputter.

She crept out of his cozy bed, vigilantly. Once she saw to it that he was still sleeping, she headed to his master bathroom. After washing her face and brushing her teeth, she slipped her naked body into one of his oversized white t-shirts and headed down the hall. She felt like cooking for him.

As soon as she had all of the ingredients and utensils she needed to make waffles from scratch, scrambled eggs, and hickory smoked bacon, he entered the kitchen, shirtless, with red plain pajama bottoms a small smile greeting her. He placed a kiss on her lips with fresh spearmint tasting breath.

"Good morning," he said.

"Good morning."

He removed the few loose strands that fell in front of her eye during her search for pots and pans. "What are you doing?"

"I'm sorry. Did I wake you with all the rummaging I was doing? You have everything so organized, but some things are too hard to reach, and I wanted to surprise you with breakfast."

"It's time for me to get up anyway." He swatted her bare ass with a loud smack. "You look quite sexy in my t-shirt."

"And no underwear…"

"I see." He chuckled. "Hey, I have an idea. Let's cook breakfast together." He scrutinized the ingredients she had out on the counter with his eyes before going to the pantry. "You don't even have everything you need to get it poppin' up in here. That's how I know you don't know what you're doing. I'm the King."

She threw her head back and laughed. "I'll let you go ahead and think that. I'm the Queen of this Kingdom."

"Must I remind you of my powers?"

A sly grin covered her face as she wagged her finger at him. "You don't play fair."

"I never play fair, but I'll give you a chance to show me what you got. I got the waffles, and you do the eggs and bacon. Cool?"

"Yup."

Working with ease, he didn't need to measure out his flour, baking powder, confectioner's sugar, butter, milk, eggs that were separated, vanilla, and just a pinch of salt. He beat the egg whites with a whisk. Seeing how he was flexing his muscles around his kitchen, she tossed a few pecans from his pantry into the maple syrup she was warming on the stove. As she watched him from behind, she couldn't help but enjoy this moment.

When his Belgian waffle was done, he topped it with her pecans, syrup, and a garnish of whipped cream. He took a fork and fed her a taste.

She closed her eyes as she chewed. "Mmmmm." She smiled widely. "Yeah... You're so dope."

He placed a kiss on her forehead. "I'm glad I have your approval."

When the food was done, they sat on his couch in the living room and ate. They shared a few laughs and drank freshly squeezed orange juice. Quadim took their plates and put them in the kitchen sink. She dug her pink frosted toes into his rug as she flipped through the TV channels to see what was on.

When he returned, he brought both of her feet to his lap and massaged them. His eyes couldn't help but take in how incredible her long bare legs looked while wearing his t-shirt. Her body was noteworthy. Even though she was thick, she was toned and fit.

She licked her lips seductively before sipping more orange juice. With a naughty expression coming to her face, a crazy sensation that tended to run up and down her spine was forming. She could feel it every time his hands moved up to her toes. The spark started in her back and shot through her in waves.

He wore a sly handsome smile as if she placed a spell on him. He had one of the sexiest smiles she had ever seen on a man, straight and white.

Suddenly, Kaori asked, "What are you doing this Saturday?"

He thought about it while rubbing her right foot. "Nothing I can think of that's concrete right now. Why? What's up?"

"There's this award dinner that I have to attend for work and I need plus one."

"… And, you want that plus one to be me?"

She smiled. "If you don't mind…"

"I don't mind, but tell me something," he said.

"What?"

"Who is he?"

She sighed and looked away. How did he know there was someone else? Taariq and Kaori had been fooling around for two years, but he didn't make her feel the way he did. She slowly found his gaze again when she answered, "My co-worker, Taariq… I used to see him and I kind of want to show you off."

Quadim stared at her while moving his hands up to her knee, contemplating the ramifications of them being seen together in front of one of her *conquests,* as she called them.

"Sure, I'll go. What should I wear?"

She stretched forward and kissed his lips before she replied, "I know you know how to dress to impress."

"You know that, huh?"

She chuckled and nodded like a schoolgirl.

Their chemistry was undeniable as they stared at one another. It was inevitable. Love was coming. He got up and made his way to the kitchen to clean up the mess. As she watched him move about his space, she found herself smiling, knowing the reason why she stayed; she loved the way he made her feel.

"Would you mind if I freshen up? Can I take the shower?"

"Sure, the shower is a little difficult. I'll turn it on for you."

They walked to his bathroom, and Quadim ran the water for her as she marveled at the sixteen showerheads lining on the two walls in front of her. The steam started to build almost immediately.

She gasped because she never seen a shower so fancy. "What kind of shower is this?"

"It's a Swiss Shower... This lever is for the hot water. This one is for the cold. You lift the bar to raise the pressure and push it down to lower the pressure. I only have one kind of body wash, so I hope Taariq won't be mad at you for smelling like me," he said with a straight face and soft eyes.

She smiled because the thought of smelling like him pleased her. "Ha ha, very funny. I don't see him anymore... I hope your *girlfriend* won't get mad that I stayed the night."

"If I had someone," he answered nonchalantly, "you would've known off the top. I don't play games." He offered her a fresh loofah and a large cotton towel as he turned on the Bose Sound Dock. Quadim lit apple scented candles for her before arranging them amicably.

"Aren't you going to shower with me?" she asked with one eyebrow raised.

"Nope. Enjoy." He pulled the door behind him to exit the bathroom again. He left her alone to bathe that beautiful body of hers and that even lovelier smile. He wondered for weeks how long it would take to get her to come over. Now that she was here, he never wanted her to leave.

***

ROUND 4

They arrived at her company's award dinner, arm in arm, on Saturday. For the first time since he initially saw Kaori walk into the bar, he felt butterflies in his stomach. She held onto his arm. He heard some man calling her name before they stopped walking. The other man looked at Quadim and Kaori as if he had seen a ghost.

"Kaori?" the guy repeated with his voice full of shock.

"Taariq…"

A bit of hurt appeared behind Taariq's eyes though his voice didn't waver as he said, "I thought you weren't coming."

She cleared her throat and answered, "I changed my mind…"

"Clearly… Are you going to introduce me to your *friend*?"

Quadim extended his hand, brandished that classic smile of his, and spoke to the dark-skinned, shorter, less muscular man that stood before them. "Quadim," he said coolly. As Taariq reached for his hand, Quadim gripped his firmly without smiling and added, "I'm her boyfriend."

Taariq was speechless and couldn't say a word. He worked so hard for two years to get Kaori to commit and now she had given some other random guy a chance. He felt his jealousy rise. When Quadim felt Taariq try to show his strength in their handshake, Quadim immediately tightened his grip until he saw the twitch in Taariq's face.

Kaori had watched the two interact, but she didn't see what the two men were actually doing. With that out of the way, Quadim turned to Kaori, taking one of her hands into his, and asked her, "Are you ready?"

She nodded slowly, feeling Taariq's confused anger darting her way through his stare. She smiled at Quadim. The fact that he referred to himself as her boyfriend didn't rub her the wrong way to her surprise. She liked it.

Kaori had no idea that Quadim wasn't only going to be the best escort for the evening, but he was also not going to play fair with *anyone* that thought they were going to take her away from him. With Quadim's charm and charismatic smile in tow, she introduced him to her coworkers. The mere mirage of him being her man cascaded down like an unexpected fog. He was quite the eye candy to every woman in the room, and she paraded him around proudly like an awarded prize medallion.

After a lovely evening with great dinner and music, the two walked out of the venue, hand in hand, towards the valet. While they waited for his car, Kaori wrapped her arms around him and smiled. She not only had more fun than she anticipated but now, they were free to do whatever they wanted to do for the rest of the night.

"What you want to do next, boyfriend?" she asked.

"How about we go back to my place?"

The car arrived before she could answer and Quadim kissed her slowly with his eyes closed while the valet held open the passenger door.

He whispered his wants to her, "You've been outvoted. You don't have a choice."

"I don't?" she whispered back. "How am I outvoted anyway?"

Quadim chuckled a bit, "Because your pussy is screaming *yes*... Can't you hear her? I can... Let's go."

And, with that, Quadim led the way for Kaori to the passenger side, made sure she buckled her seatbelt, and softly closed the door to his A7 before tipping the valet.

This man, this man, this man... was moving his way into her life and without delay. He made it so hard for her to breathe half of the time.

When he strolled to the driver's seat, he saw Taariq emerge with a semi-snide look on his face. Quadim simply raised one eyebrow and tilted his head before he got in, and knew, without a shadow of a doubt, that he would fight for her if it came to it and he would enjoy it.

As Kaori took off her heels and stretched out her legs, her dress shimmered underneath the passing streetlamps. "The most beautiful shoes always hurt the worst... Seems like it anyway."

"You women have it hard enough, but I do love those shoes on you."

While he drove, she reached over, smiled at him, and rubbed his head lightly. The back of her fingers of her left hand followed the freshly trimmed beard until she reached his chin and they stopped at a red light.

He took his eyes off the road for a brief moment to observe her hint of arousal.

Kaori licked her candy painted lips slowly before she muttered, "Come closer."

When he started in, she pulled her right hand, the one she had been using to play with herself, from under her dress and placed them to his lips. The warmth of her dew turned cool almost instantly, but the aroma of things to come lit a fire underneath his already burning desires for her. Silently, with his eyes, she had been given the choice of how she wanted to cum once they got back to his house.

"I want to be on top," she said, reading his mind.

Her selection noted, Quadim didn't say another word about it as he proceeded through the intersection once the light was green, which made Kaori, even more, anxious for them to arrive. The drive to his home was a mix of inebriated thoughts, subtle laughs, and pleasurable aches with a lead foot leading the way.

She smiled, and her heart fluttered. She was going to have to admit to her friends that she had lost the fight inside of Quadim's ring of fire. She was in love.

Niyah Moore is an award-winning author with more than twenty published works to her credit. A Sacramento, California native, Niyah's love affair with the written word began early. By the age of nine she was fully immersed in the possibilities of prose. Under the subtle urging and guidance of her literary mentors, Niyah embarked on a professional writing career.

A true contemporary artist, Niyah's foray into the literary world began in 2007 with the social media platform Myspace, where she submitted her writing to be included in select anthologies. Niyah has since secured multiple independent publishing deals, as well as having been included in several anthologies such as: *Zane's Busy Bodies: Chocolate Flava 4, Anna J's Lies Told in the Bedroom, Heat of the Night,* and *Mocha Chocolate: Taste a Piece of Ecstasy.* Her anthology, *Patron on Ice* was recently released on Amazon.

After seven years of self-publishing and honing her craft, Niyah stepped into the role of CEO and Publisher launching Ambiance Books in February 2015. Ambiance Books has signed eighteen authors to date. Niyah's journey has been paved with determination and drive. For more information on Niyah visit www.niyahmoore.com

ACT II: UNEXPECTED LOVE

In Between These Walls
Terrie Branch

"Don't waste your love on somebody who doesn't value it."
-William Shakespeare

A very tense mood took over the room after Tracey's husband had nearly extracted her eye completely from her head. Devastated by his actions, she now lay on the floor in a corner in their kitchen in the fetal position crying. Not knowing if he had left or not, she didn't want to let her two-year-old go; assuming that the rage that her husband Tim was on was not yet over. She didn't know how he would react to the baby approaching him. Being a kid, he didn't understand. So like any other child, he would think it was okay to do the things that he normally did on any other day. As they both lay there, the baby looked at her and turned his lip down as if he was about to cry himself. Not old enough to realize what was going on, but nevertheless able to notice that the mood overall was a deplorable one. So she gripped onto his bottom holding him trying to keep them both safe. She heard the slamming of doors and other things as he continued whatever it was that he was doing at the other end of the home. She sat there wondering if it was even a good idea to get up at this point.

He walked into the kitchen and opened the refrigerator and grabbed a drink. He disregarded the fact that the baby and Tracey were still lying where he left them. He stormed out of the kitchen and into another area of the house. Tim had always been a cheater long before Tracey, ever met him; she simply wasn't aware of it. He usually wooed any and every one with his smooth ways, and that pretty much got him all that he desired.

Before the attack, Tracey, and the baby had just returned to the house. She wasn't yet cognizant of what was about to occur.

"Hey, honey. " Tracey said, trying to kiss her husband.

"What's up?" He said as he halfway pecked her on the lips. She noticed that he was less affectionate with her lately. She assumed that he might have had a bad work week or perhaps just in a bad mood due to something else. She knew that she hadn't done anything wrong, so she went about her business and tried to remain clear of him until he was back to himself.

Tracey started cleaning up when she noticed their son picked up a juice bottle and was just about to drink it when she noticed that something was in the bottom of the bottle. Tracey reached over and grabbed it and her son began to cry.

"No baby... This is dirty. Mommy will get you another one."

"What the hell is this?" She said looking into the bottom of the sixteen-ounce clear bottle. She scurried into the living room, looking for her husband, to show him that something was in the drink and to inform him that their son almost drunk it.

These damn beverage companies need to be more careful when packaging up their shit she said to herself.

Once she realized that Tim wasn't in the living room, she turned to head to the bedroom. On the way to the bedroom, she noticed what appeared to be a letter sitting on the top of the entertainment cabinet. She sat down the bottle and grabbed the letter. .

Bitch, I hope you enjoy the spit in your fucking drink and yes, I have been in your damn house. Your husband is fucking me and doesn't want your stupid ass! Before long he is going to leave your ass and be with me! I plan on making your life a living hell up until that point!!!

Tracey stood there for a second in shock. The thought of Tim having a bitch in her house pissed her off to the max and to add injury to insult, the trick spit in her drink and her son almost drank it. Now shit was starting to make sense. The rejection and all the late nights claiming he was working extra hours was a damn lie. Tracey trusted him and couldn't believe what she had just read. She grabbed the bottle and stormed into the bedroom, fuming with rage. "Tim, what is this shit?" She asked holding up the letter and the bottle.

Even though she was mad that he had cheated on her and nonetheless in her home, but she was even more upset that their son had almost consumed some bitch's spit!

Once he saw the note, all the color left out his face. He looked from the letter to the bottle and instantly got defensive.

"What the fuck are you talking about?"

"This letter that your bitch left for me and her spit that our son almost drank!"

"I haven't had no fucking body in this damn house!" He said and walked past her brushing up against her so hard that he almost knocked her down.

She followed behind him.

"Well explain this letter, Tim!" She said, demanding answers. She was so upset with herself that she didn't pick up on his cheating ways from the beginning. Maybe she didn't see it because she was a little naïve, but wanted their relationship to work, so she kept giving him the benefit of the doubt.

He went into the front room. "Look, stop fucking nagging me!" He pronounced in an angry tone.

She picked up her son, who looked like he wanted to cry from all the screaming and hollering. "I guess this damn letter just magically landed in our house, huh?" Tracey said, getting even more upset that he was lying to her face. The disrespect, the lies, and deceit had been taken to another level!

"Tim, the bitch spit in the drinks in the kitchen. You are not concerned that our child almost drank that shit?" She continued.

Tim continued to move about the house, ignoring her, causing her to become even more annoyed. She sat their son down on the chair and followed him, looking for answers that she already knew the answers to, seeking closure.

"Get the fuck out my face with this shit man!" He yelled at her. He knew he was wrong, but he felt if he turned the tables on her that it would make him feel less guilty about it. He didn't care about Tracey's feelings at the moment, all he could think about was beating the fuck out of his side chick for leaving a note like that and for the fact that his son almost drank her spit. He knew his relationship with Tracey was over a long time ago, but he loved his son deeply, and the fact that he was almost harmed by his carelessness and that bitch's selfishness had him furious.

"Why would you do that Tim?" She inquired, starting to weep.

"Do what? I told your ass I didn't do shit! Your ass making up shit, to start arguments, man! You probably wrote that shit yourself. Trying to start some bullshit!"

"So, I guess I spit in our son's drink for attention too, huh? I heard the rumors about how you have been fucking around on me since we have been together, but I gave you the benefit of the doubt! The bad thing about it is that everyone knew it but me! That shit is so fucking embarrassing!" She yelled.

"All that shit in your damn mind, man!" He said followed by a sarcastic laugh.

Tracey became more upset as he seemed to find his infidelity humorous.

"I hate your stupid ass!" She yelled at the top of her lungs.

"Bitch, Get the fuck out of here with that shit!" He said just before hawking up a wad of spit and releasing it in Tracey's face. She could see his rage was building and knew that the best thing to do was to leave it alone and decide at this point, what she needed to do to get out of this situation or if it was even worth working to repair.

"You know what, fuck it! Fuck you and this marriage! I'm tired of this. I don't deserve this shit! I'm leaving!" Tracey stated as she wiped the spit from her face.

She turned and attempted to walk away. Before she could leave, Tim hit her in the face and grabbed her face with his hand. The pain was excruciating. She stood motionless for a moment. She felt a warm sensation easing down the right side of her face. In panic mode, Tracey grabbed a hold of his fingers and tried to get him to let go of her face, but he wasn't giving in at all. She started to cry harder, begging and pleading with him to let go; he wouldn't. Tim wasn't showing any remorse for what he was doing. She could feel his grip on becoming more intense. She knew if he didn't release his hand that she would probably lose an eye.

Their son had now gotten down from the chair and was heading in the direction of his dad. He grabbed a hold of Tim's leg, and Tracey could feel his grip lessening. Finally, he released this grip shoving her towards the kitchen, so hard she nearly fell. Her face got hot and started throbbing; she knew it wouldn't be long before the swelling started. She was too scared to go to the restroom to take a look at her face, so she stayed in the kitchen and dropped to the floor in tears. Seeing her fall to the floor, her son walked over to her. She didn't want her son to look at her face, so she grabbed her son and pulled him into her chest hiding her face from him. She knew Tim didn't feel any guilt for doing this to her.

Tracey couldn't understand how he could treat her this way for no apparent reason. She considered herself the ideal wife. She made sure he came home to a clean home and a hot meal every day. Attempting to keep their marriage fresh, she planned quality time alone and on other occasions with other couples. She would attempt to communicate throughout their relationship, but he would always pass up her efforts, telling Tracey that she was nagging, which was his way of brushing her off.

Now, she was balled up in the fetal position with her son, weeping wondering where it all went wrong. Was she not attractive enough? Was she not doing something right? No, she tried to make it work. However, if a man hasn't matured despite the age, it wasn't going to ever work. What Tracey couldn't see right now was that it would take a great man to give her the love that she deserve and Tim wasn't that man!

Tracey started to have thoughts about her past relationships, as she lay there crying.

How could I keep choosing men like this? I'm such a good woman. Why do I continually end up in situations like this? I can't continue to live like this. I have to get away from this!

Thinking of how Lawaun, her ex-boyfriend was mentally abusive. This situation was like an instant replay of her past relationships. Although Lawaun never hit her, the cheating and the lying is what caused their relationship to go on a downward spiral. From cheating and staying out nightly with other females all night. Now Tracey and Lawaun didn't reside with one another, however, moments that she needed him there he wasn't anywhere to be found.

After Lawaun, she waited about three years before starting another relationship. She ended up falling for Tim and was determined to make her relationship work. Listening to him, call her out her name, it all seemed so familiar to her past.

Tracey was tired...

Is all this shit my fault? No, no, it's not my fault. Maybe it is if I had stood up for myself by not letting anyone step over my morals and standards that I have in a relationship. Maybe if I hadn't accepted it from the beginning... Tracey continued asking herself. At this moment, she realized that it wasn't too late to stand up. She wouldn't allow Tim to treat her this way any longer. She was a prize. She was the key player. Until she loved and respected herself enough to walk away, she would remain in an unhealthy relationship. Upon hearing him slam the front door, she got up off the floor. She headed to the room and picked up the phone and called her sister.

"Hey, sis…" She said weeping. "Can I stay with you for a while?" She continued.

"What's wrong? Did he hit you again?" Shelia yelled into the phone.

"No… I'm okay! I promise. We have to leave here before he comes back."

"Yes! Yes, you can. Do you want me to come get you?" Shelia asked.

"No.. I can drive there, but I have to get out of here before he comes back," She said looking over her shoulder to make sure he hadn't come back in.

"Okay, If you're not here in the next thirty minutes, I'm coming to get you. I'm bringing Mark and Brian too!" Shelia said, mentioning her brothers' names.

Tracey hung up and rushed to get the baby and her clothes. She went to the refrigerator and grabbed some of the baby's things. She knew his routine. He would come home, curse, fight, then leave the house, only to return later and makeup. He would expect them to brush the incident under the rug. Now, she was tired and needed to do something about it.

*****

Awakened by a gentle kiss on her forehead, Tracey realized her past was now a distant memory. All the mental and physical abuse was over now. She was finally in a healthy relationship with a real man. She never thought that she would find a love of this kind. She thought her chances of having happiness were slim to none; that's until years later when she met Dashuan. After her relationships with Tim and Lawaun, Tracey had given up on love.

She reminisced on how her Prince Charming Dashuan came into her life unexpectedly. During this time she was solely focused on her career and her son,

111

since the turmoil of the vehement relationships had ended. She didn't want to trust her heart in the hands of another man, just yet. At that time, she felt she just wasn't ready. Her friends continuously tried to hook her up, only to be disappointed when Tracey rejected them. She loved her friends, but she just wanted them to respect the fact that she wanted to wait for love. She knew that they meant well and only wanted to see her happy.

On this particular day, Tracey sat in a small café with Lisa and Angie, two of her closest friends at happy hour.

"Hey, chicas! How are you?" Angie greeted the other girls.

"Hey there!" Tracey and Lisa said in unison.

Lisa reached for the menu and handed the girls theirs. "So what's been going on? Lisa said while looking at the menu.

"Girl, I am getting prepared for the Bahamas. I have been planning this trip with my family for the reunion for a while. I wish you guys would've considered coming along!"Angie said.

"Nothing much here just work," Tracey said.

The ladies ordered their drinks and continued to make small talk amongst themselves until the waitress brought their drinks.

"You guys ready to order?" The waitress asked while giving them their drinks.

"Yes, we are. Angie answered for them both. Then the ladies placed their orders. They continued the conversation amongst the three of them while waiting for their food.

"Hey Angie!" yelled a very handsome guy, Tracey had never seen before, as he came over to the table. She tried not to make it obvious that she was moved by him. In her past, looks had been a downfall for her, because evidently they thought they were all that! She looked down as if she was fishing something out of her purse, but it was too late. Lisa had already picked up on her attraction to him.

"Hey, you!" Angie said, returning the hug that the guy was giving her.

"I'm sorry ladies, excuse my manners. How are you?" Dashuan asked, in a deep baritone voice.

"Fine…" They both said.

"Girls, This is Dashuan. He works with me. I guess you could say he is one of my buddies." Angie said smiling and looking over at him.

"Please to meet you all," He said as he reached out to shake each one of the lady's hands.

His beautiful smile was enough to woo any woman. Lisa was married already and didn't have any interest, but she didn't mind looking at a nice piece of eye candy.

Tracey quickly checked herself.

Tracey pull yourself together. You have already been through enough dealing with these pretty boys. He's fine and all but looks can be deceiving. Stay focused on what matters, she told herself.

"Tracey is single," Angie said suddenly, almost causing Tracey to choke on her drink.

He looked over at her and quickly responded to Angie, "Oh yeah? Don't put her on the spot. Hey, she may not want her business out there like that."

"I'm just saying..." Angie said with a sly grin while Tracey sat shaking her head.

Tracey and Lisa sat listening to Dashaun and Angie talk for a few minutes before the waitress came back with their meals.

"Well, you ladies enjoy your meals and it was nice to meet you. " He said before excusing himself from the table. The ladies blessed their meals and began to eat and enjoyed the rest of the evening.

Two months later...

Tracey sat on the beach catching a little sun while her son played. She enjoyed being at the beach. It was so peaceful. Just relaxing and occasionally picking up a magazine browsing through it.

Her son played around with two other kids on the beach around the same age. They threw a football back and forth until they lost control of it in the wind. He came over to her with a sad look on his face. He knew what the rules were about going too close to the water. So Tracey decided to get up and get it for the kids. Just as she was about to, someone else grabbed it for the boys. As this handsome man turned around, she noticed that it was Dashuan from the café. She felt a little embarrassed after remembering how her friend Angie had painted this lonely old single woman picture of her to Dashuan.

"Don't I remember you?" He asked, still in the deepest voice she had ever heard.

She smiled and shook her head and answered, "Yes.."
Standing there not knowing what to say, she looked
surprised to see him.

"Angie's friend from the café right?" He asked.

"Yes.." She said

"I know that you were a bit embarrassed by the
way Angie threw you out there like that, huh?" He asked.

"Yeah, she is a bit pushy, but it's all out of love, I
guess. She said giggling and shaking her head all at the
same time.

"Ask me how I know, though!" He said smiling.

"How?" She asked.

"Because she does the same thing to me!" He said,
and they both burst out into laughter.

"What?" Tracey asked.

"Yeah, I've been single for a while. I've been
through a few bad relationships myself. I mean I don't

know your reason and all, but speaking from my experience. So I have just been getting to know me and focusing on me. I mean I want another relationship eventually, but I don't want to force it." He said as he walked her in the direction of her beach chair. "Do you mind if I talk to you for a minute?" He asked.

She looked in the direction of her chair, then back at him. "No, I don't mind. I only have one chair, though." She said.

I'm cool. We are at the beach. I can sit on the sand. Do you think that I would let not having a chair to sit in, stop me from sitting and talking with a woman as beautiful as you?" He asked.

She smiled, and they sat down and talked. Little did Tracey know this man would end up being her soul mate.

***

Months later...

Meeting him through a mutual friend and them hitting it off; Suddenly became a dream come true for her. After seeing one another for a while, they decided to date exclusively. Soon after, he proposed to Tracey bringing tears to her eyes. Her family and friends loved their union. Everyone could feel the love that they shared. It was obvious to the world.

This man rarely allowed her to remove her shoes without his assistance. She could now feel what it felt like to be truly loved and respected. After quite some time of dating, this man still awed her. He professed, provided, and protected Tracey. He took care of her and with that being said; she knew she had to take care of him.

As she lay, he gently rubbed her forehead and looked at her with admiration in his eyes. Tracey could feel his love through his touch, through his long stare. She felt safe in his arms, and that was one of the greatest feelings a woman could ever have.

"I love you, baby…" Dashaun said to her, sending a sensation through her torso and a signal straight to her vagina walls.

"I love you too baby!" She said just before reaching upward and rubbing his face; she guided his face to hers. She planted her tongue deep into his mouth, rotating it. She had to please this man.

She then pushed the covers back and slid underneath them. Sliding his boxer briefs back, she placed his erect penis into her mouth. She began to enjoy every inch of his very well endowed manhood. She put his hands on both sides of it, massaging his dick with both. Moaning and sucking… Moaning and sucking… She devoured his delicious penis. She loved this man, and that took the enjoyment of it to another level by kissing it in preparation to their lovemaking. She treated it as if it was the appetizer leading to their sex!

His toes curled as she moved faster and faster…

"Baby I want your dick inside of me…" She said.

He said nothing as he pulled her up looking her deep into her eyes. He ushered her to lie down. He removed his shirt because he wasn't going to allow anything to disrupt their lovemaking.

He lifted her legs and placed them on his shoulders...

She jumped slightly as his long thick manhood entered her tight vagina wall.

"Mmm... Oh, baby!" She said.

"Fuck!" He said, feeling the wetness surrounding his dick.

Pushing himself in and out of her in a rhythmic manner as she creamed all over his dick. He picked up the pace as his dick began to feel the benefits of a wet pussy... and not just any but HIS pussy!

He slowed down a little avoiding a release of his milky substance inside of her. He couldn't resist. Grabbing her nipples with his teeth, he tugged on them just before kissing and sucking on them.

She threw her pussy at him, wanting him to have it all.

"Take your pussy, baby! Take it!" She yelled at him as he began to fuck her harder.

"Give that shit to me! Dammit! Ugh!" He said as she sunk her nails into his back! Pounding his dick into her, he stroked and stroked her pussy.

Her eye released a single tear as the feelings she had for him and he had for her.

"Oh, baby! I'm cumming!" She screamed. She grabbed a hold of his strong, deep dark chocolate back. Never wanting to let go of this man!

They climaxed together…

To be alone in a relationship is not ideal… but when you finally enter a relationship where both parties exude the same type of love for one another it can be a very powerful relationship! Building on the same foundation,

honesty, loyalty, and communication; all key points in a
healthy relationship...

Terri Branch is a published author of four books; one with
Authorhouse Publishing and the *Gotta Be Sheisty Series*
under Kiki Swinson Publications. Her upcoming releases
include *Choose your Poison* and *Mr. CEO* with Shaunta Kenerly
Presents. She also was recently interviewed for *Writer's Digest* and
they will be releasing a new publication in 2016 that will include
Terrie's Signature quotes. She was recently selected as one of UBAWA
Top 100 Authors of 2015. She was featured in *Pen'Ashe Magazine*
February 2016 issue.

Taking pride in being a single mother of two sons, she continues to
walk by faith while standing and believing in God's word. She is a
motivational speaker, entrepreneur, commissioned Notary Public,
and Cosmetologist/Barber Instructor. In 2014, she launched her very
own cosmetic line, *SheerBoss Cosmetics* and partnered opening
Perfect Styles Beauty and Barber School. For more information about
Terri https://www.facebook.com/terrie.branch

ACT III:

INSEPARABLE

LOVE

More Than Friends

Xyla Turner

"I love thee with a love that shall not die, till the sun grows cold and the stars grow old." -William Shakespeare

SECTION I: TAY

Tay watched Stacy put the can on the top shelf. Her shirt rose slightly as her bronze colored lower stomach peeked at him, and she had on that short flirty skirt. They were at his apartment after work, like they always went on Fridays. Stacy wanted to have some peace and quiet because her roommate always had some shit with her. A week ago, their argument almost turned into a physical fight which caused Tay to throw Stacy over his shoulder and drag her ass back to his apartment.

Everyone said that the two of us should just get together, but for years, we both said the same thing. 'We're just cool.' Even my uncle, who don't get into nobody's business said that even a blind man could see that I was into her, and he even called me a pussy for not saying something. He wouldn't even let me explain.

"Unc, you don't understand," I attempted to say.

"Fuck you mean, I don't understand?" He shifted his weight on the left side and raised an eyebrow. "I'm old enough to eat cornbread and not choke. Fuck you mean. Man up and stop being a bitch. That gal is going to leave yo ass for some other dude, then what?"

That would never happen because I wouldn't let her.

Stacy and I met in high school as we were in the same Algebra class with Mr. Sievini. My man didn't teach for shit and always had pop quizzes. Most of us in his class struggled with math, and we still do to this day. That was because this man decided he wanted to teach Algebra one and two, causing us to have his class for two straight years. Stacy was always vocal about her dislike for him and his teaching method, which he simply didn't do. So was I and to his face, which is why Stacy and I were on speaking terms. We had a mutual understanding, and that respect did not go beyond that Algebra class. Well, not until I realized she lived around the corner from my cousin Izzy and Shane, did we develop a sense of rapport with one another.

She was cool, never flirted or any of that shit with us. Stacy had her friends, but occasionally she'd come over and play video games or shoot the shit with my aunt. Izzy thought she was gay; my aunt thought she liked Izzy, who was gay and Shane didn't care but what I did know was that she didn't like me. That was fine at 19, but we were 24, and this shit was getting old. She was a great friend, and as much as I wanted to keep it that way, I wouldn't live my life being this close to her and knowing that was the closest I'd ever get.

Philly had changed a lot over the years, and so had the rent. My job with UPS was good, and I had all the flexibility that I wanted. Therefore, I didn't mind rooming with Shane even though his girlfriend was hinting towards them getting a place of their own. Andrea and he had been together for almost ten years. She did more than hint at him popping the big question; she bought the damn ring.

Who the fuck does that?

Shane thought it was weird, made her take it back and had one of those coming to Jesus moments with her. Telling her that when he was ready, he would propose and not a minute sooner. That happened two years ago, and he still hadn't. Served her ass right. Even Stacy said that was some bullshit.

On the weekends when she wasn't working at the airport, she would come and hang out with us. Most of her friends had gone to college, moved or had boyfriends and left all girl stuff for the birds. Therefore, when she was free, she was here.

Stacy bent back down to get another can of string beans and stretched to put it in the top cabinet. She was 5'9 which was perfect for me since I was six foot three, fitting right into me. She was not skinny and not obese,

128

but just right. Probably a 10/12 in size. Hips, ass, and her breast were C-cups. She was perfect.

Stop.

I couldn't keep thinking of her like that. I was losing my mind. It's her on my mind when I go to bed, when I wake up with my dick hard as a fucking rock, when I release in the shower and every damn minute of every day. Especially Fridays, when she would come over and give me her smile with those sexy ass lips. Her pink pouty bottom lip and skin-colored, full top lip. I want to bite them and hear her moan. Louder than when she hums to the Häagen-Dazs Chocolate Peanut Butter ice cream that I keep stocked especially for her. I want her perfect body to writhe under me, as I moved into her.

I can't keep doing this shit to myself. My fucking Uncle was right. I *was* a pussy.

"Look, Stacy," I started. "Got some shit to …"

"Look at me!" Stacy exclaimed as she shook her head. "I'm so mad; I'm putting away your goddamn groceries."

"I have no complaints," I replied.

And I didn't because watching her body move, bend and stretch like that made me want to put my hands all over it to make it move the way I wanted. I knew I could because she was perfect for me in every way. These feelings I had for her were taking over and to the point that my daydreams seemed so vivid and my night dreams were only a tease.

In my mind, I could just feel her under me as I placed both hands on her curved waist, moving them up towards her buxom breasts and leaning into a whisper, "I got you."

"Tay?" her small voice called in the tiny kitchen breaking my trance.

"Yeah," I murmured.

Her smell traveled up my nostrils, deeming me intoxicated.

"Why are you touching me like that?" Her voice was still small.

OH SHIT!

Blinking my eyes, I looked down to see my hands were on her hips pressing her ass into my hard dick, and my lips were inches away from her ear.

Holy fuck!

SECTION II: STACY

Oh my God.

Oh my God.

OH MY GOD!

Tay Johnson had his hands on me. He needed to get off and back away. What the fuck was he doing?

"Oh, uh." His hands slowly peeled off my body.

The heat from his touch scorched my already hot body. We had been cool for years, and the main reason I fucked with him was because he didn't try anything. *Ever.* I never dressed overly sexy because I didn't want the attention or the eyes of any guy and especially Tay. He made it clear he wasn't interested in high school. The man wouldn't even acknowledge me outside of Algebra class. I, all but, befriended his family so I could get closer to the broody man.

We'd never done anything or even hinted towards it, so in my mind – I just thought he and the possibility of us were off limits.

To him, anyway.

"Tay," I whispered as I turned around.

"Fuck," he hissed. "I can't keep doing this shit."

"What?" my face was hot with embarrassment and annoyed with his words.

His fingers ran through his hair with his eyebrows pushed together in the center, causing his worry lines to deepen. Tay only every looked like this when he was about to lose control. Before I realized it, my hand reached up to smooth the lines on his forehead. His eyes widened in surprise and his mouth slightly parted.

"Keep doing what?" I asked, continuing to rub my thumb up and down his wrinkled brows.

He grabbed my wrist and tried to stop me, but I stepped into his personal space and lifted my other hand to his shoulder. Tay's pained eyes looked at me, and he murmured, "This. I can't keep doing this. You're fucking killing me."

His grip tightened on my wiggling wrist as he held my arm in mid-air. In an attempt to trick him, I relaxed my hand thinking that he'd let me g,o but he pulled my hand up to his face and held it there for a few seconds. My hand cupped his jaw as my fingers strummed his ears. Right before my eyes, he turned and kissed my palm causing my entire body to come alive like a Christmas tree. My nipples were instantly hard, the ache between my legs intensified and the hair on my arm stood at attention.

"Do you want to know what you do to me?" I blurted, apparently not authorizing what the fuck was coming out of my mouth.

Tay's brows raised as he slowly turned from my palm and those brown mesmerizing eyes bore into me. He was reading me like a book, his eyes darting back and forth, up and down looking for clues to solve the puzzle. My other hand moved upward and gripped his neck. His body stilled as his gaze seemed to light a flame within me.

To my dismay and embarrassment, he slowly lifted his right hand, removed my arm from around his neck and took a step away from me.

"What are you doing?" I asked.

"Saving us both," he murmured and left his own apartment.

SECTION III: TAY

The fall breeze blew through me like I was not six foot three, two hundred and twenty pounds and solid as a fucking rock. Half of my stature were compliments of my job of manual labor, and the other half of it was I wanted to stay in shape. It wasn't because I overheard Stacy say to her friend that she liked guys that were strong and solid.

That was not the reason that I had a strength training workout regimen that I stuck with for years.

"Where the fuck are you going?" I heard a familiar voice break through my thoughts.

"Shit, sorry. What's up?" I nodded towards Shane.

"Where are you going? It's cold as shit out here, and you're in a t-shirt, ball shorts, and sneakers?" Shane was looking at me like I was fresh from the mental hospital.

"Look, Stacy is at the house. Some shit went down, and I needed some air."

"What kind of shit?" He was standing and looking at me with squinted eyes.

"I, uh," I started. This was fucking embarrassing, but he'd hear it anyway. "I fucked up man. Before I knew what had happened, my hands were around her waist, and I was pushing up on her. Then," I sighed. "I just had to get the fuck out of there."

"What!" he exclaimed. "Bout goddamn time. Damn! What did she do?" He asked as he looked like he was about to jump up and down with excitement.

Shane didn't do shit like that. Get excited or jump. He was pretty straight-laced, so to see him overjoyed about me feeling up on our old friend was a little weird.

"What?" I asked in confusion. "We're friends, man. That's what it's been, and that's what it'll be."

"What!?!" His head reared back as his lip turned up. "I'm beginning to think you're the pussy your uncle keeps calling you. Here I was defending you and saying, when it was time, you'd step up. But now," he stretched his hand palm up towards me and said, "presented with the opportunity, you turn and walk away to get some fucking air. I smell, puh, puh, puh, PUSSY!" He barked.

"Fuck you, Shane."

"No, man. Fuck you!" He stepped to me. "I'm going to make myself scarce and stay with Drea. The report I better hear tomorrow is that you and Stacy either came to a resolution, fucked or something. I'm sick of y'all shit. Y'all have been dancing, staring and pussy-footin' around for a while now. Seal the deal. Cause what you don't want is someone to snatch her right from under you and you think you're mad now. The worst thing you can have is regrets."

Fuck.

He was right. He was so fucking right. My uncle has said the same thing, almost and they were both right. The thought of another man even touching her had me seeing red. That *couldn't...*

No.

That *wouldn't* happen, ever.

Shane raised one eyebrow at me, but I did not catch anything else he did because I had turned around and was headed back home.

I had to claim what was mine.

The door slammed open causing Stacy to yell out in surprise. She was standing in the foyer looking lost, confused and even had wetness around her eyes.

Fuck!

I did not even think of what she might have felt; I was stuck in my head. Forcing the door shut with my foot, I moved towards her and cornered against the hallway door.

"Now what was it that I do to you?" I growled.

Our noses were touching as I hovered over her. She stared into my eyes with no fear but what looked like *relief.*

"You make me want things I shouldn't," she breathed against my lips.

"Why shouldn't you want them?" I grabbed her wrists so they were up near her head as I pinned them against the wall.

"Because you don't have those same feelings about me?" she said.

"Wanna bet?" I nipped her bottom, pouty lip.

Pressing my body against hers, I kissed my way from her mouth to her ear and whispered, "You feel that, sweetheart? This is me every night thinking about you in every way in my life."

"Taaayyy," she breathed in my ear.

"I'm here." I bit her earlobe. "Not going anywhere and never letting you go."

I let go of her wrists, then slightly bent down to lift her around my waist. That flirty little skirt rode up her body, causing me to have my hands on her bare ass because her thong was hidden between her tight globes.

"Mine," I growled against her lips.

"Yes, Tay." She moaned. "Yours."

Son of a bitch.

What the fuck had I been waiting on? All this goddamn time and here she was with her long legs wrapped around me with those thick thighs hugging my waist. This was the moment I had been waiting on for what felt like years.

This very moment and I knew exactly what to do first. I moved us so her back was against the wall and I took her lips softly at first, and then I took advantage of her surprise and slid my tongue into her hot mouth. She moaned, sending chills down my body and straight to my dick. Her mouth opened for me, and I invaded her completely. Nipping her lips, twirling our tongues, and taking anything I could. I kissed her until we were both out of breath. She tasted like a sweet nectar, tailor-made for my liking. All of my senses were heightened as I tuned into her rubbing her wet pussy on me. My ball shorts weren't hiding anything, which meant I could feel everything.

"Taaayyy," she moaned in my ear as she pulled my locs.

Fuck.

Quickly, I turned and headed towards my room. There was no way that I would last long because this was a long time coming and fuck that but she would come before me.

Throwing her on the bed, I ripped off my shirt from the back and threw it on the floor. Placing my knee on the bed, I rolled up her skirt, so it was around her waist. There she laid in a pink thong that had bows strategically placed on each hip. Her eyes were low, a smirk was planted on her face, and those inviting lips were parted. The thong was cute, but that shit had to go.

My two fingers slid underneath it, grazing her scorching skin and ripped the thong off.

"Tay," she gasped.

I ignored her, reached for that little ass shirt and ripped it off too. When I went to snatch off her bra, she held her hand out and said, "Wait, I got it. Ripping all my shit. How the fuck am I going to get home?"

"You're not going home," I said with no fear, no anguish and not a chance of taking it back.

My hands cupped her as so I could move her further on the bed. She managed to get her bra off, so I feasted on her supple brown nipples while she moaned and writhed under me. Her hands had my locs wrapped around them as she pulled, guided and urged me to take what's mine.

Lifting my head and causing her darkened nipple to pop out of my mouth, I looked at her and said, "I've waited so long for this."

One side of her mouth lifted in a smirk as she pulled me down, so my mouth hovered over hers. "Not as long as I have."

Then she flipped me over and planted her lips on mine. Her legs caged me in as she sat down on my crotch and started to sway her hips over my already hard dick. Then she began to kiss her way down to my chest. Motherfucker, she was going there. I wanted to stop her and tell her she didn't have too, but, fuck if I didn't want those lips wrapped around me, taking me in and out of her hot mouth.

"Stacy," I managed to groan.

Her eyes stayed on me as she wiggled down and pulled off my shorts.

Fuck.

My man was at attention, and if I knew she was mine, the look in her eyes knew I was hers.

Stacy wrapped both hands around my dick and began to move up and down. Then she licked the pre-cum from the head, causing me to knife up and catch it all.

"Take it all, sweetheart," I urged her.

I was on the edge, and this shit had to be done so I could take my time with her for the rest of the night.

Her lips wrapped around my dick, and she began to move up and down, taking me in as far as she could. I wrapped my hand around her hair and guided her further. A few times, I held her there as I fucked her mouth. She took it all like the good girl she was.

What the fuck had I been waiting for?

My body was on edge, and I needed her in the worst way. Twisting my body around, I flipped her over, so I was on top. She yelped in surprise, but I nipped her bottom lip while I wrapped my arms around her thighs, baring her sweet wet pussy to me. Moving my head down, I begin to massage her nub as she screamed out my name. Her breathing was ragged, and she kept moving her hips causing me to pin her down.

"Stop, sweetheart. I got you." I whispered as I pulled her nub into my mouth.

One finger slid inside with some resistance. My girl was tight, and that alone caused my dick to swell even more beyond its limit. I added another finger and felt her body tense from the invasion. My tongue continued to massage her clit while I curled my fingers to reach her spot.

"Fuuuuccckkk," she moaned.

Stacy's back arched, and she hit the bed with a thud. My tongue and fingers kept at it while she swirled her hips into me.

"Yes," she hissed. "Fuck, yessss."

She was close; I could feel the tightness in her body as her back went straight. I flicked her taut nub a few more times with my tongue, and she yelled out her release. It was a hard orgasm that I wanted to ride out with her.

Moving quickly, I pulled up, so my knees were in the middle of her legs. Each arm had one thigh draped over it, and I slowly lined my hard as steel dick directly in front of her wet pussy.

"Put me in, baby," I instructed.

She was still coming down from her orgasm, but she did what I told her to do. Once she worked the head in, I was able to push through. There were some moments where I saw the discomfort but then her face relaxed and as I moved in her, she started to scratch my chest and instruct me to go faster.

Bossy thing.

Some of my locs had come out of the elastic holder and were hanging down. Stacy moved them behind my ear and pulled me down, so my face was inches away from hers.

"Faster," she mouthed.

Lifting to one side, I pulled her leg, so it was on top of the other as I powered into her faster and faster.

"Like that, baby." I was about to lose it. "Fuck you like that?"

"Yess, Tay," She yelled. "Come in me, baby."

Holy shit.

That was it.

Two more thrust and I growled my release out and came inside her tight pussy. Stacy fell back on the bed, and I partially collapsed on her.

"That's what I'm talking about," she said sounding as if she had already faded away. "Been waiting for this for like ever."

Xyla Turner was born and raised in Brooklyn, New York. She is an avid reader of romance novels and a sucker for sassy females and dominant males. She is a high school educator and a groovy Aunt. Outside of reading, Xyla likes to spend time with her family and friends and travel. She writes different genres, but her favorite is romance. Xyla has written over ten novels and participated in many anthologies. Her anthology, *Women Withstanding All* is coming soon!

Xyla has her Bachelor's degree in Education and Masters in Education Administration. For more information about Xyla, please visit www.xylaturner.com

The Black Swan
Phylicia G.

"The course of true love never did run smooth."

-Phylicia G.

June 10, 2000

It was 10 a.m. at Greenville High School auditorium for the class of 2000. Tammy Groves and Terrance James, who were best friends, same birth months, the same dreams, but shared different lives, were getting ready to walk across the stage and step into the real world.

Tammy smiled as she gave a standing ovation to her best friend as he walked across the stage to receive his diploma and many other awards during the ceremony. Terrance ran to his mother first who stood by the stage waiting to hug her son and then he ran straight to Tammy.

"WE DID IT!" Terrance and Tammy hugged each other.

They both enlisted in the military. Tammy always found an interest in planes and helicopters so she joined the air force. Terrance was the protector at any cost so he joined the Marines. Terrance always made sure Tammy did what she was supposed to do and not what she wanted to do; he kept her on her toes. Mainly because Terrance was always somewhere near to pick her up when she fell. Tammy lacked the ability to lift herself up after her mother passed away.

Tammy was ten years old when her mother overdosed on heroin. She was then sent to live in a group home in Greenville, South Carolina. Tammy and Terrance met at the school bus stop when he defended her in a fight. They shared a seat on the bus and became best friends from that day forward. Not developing quickly like the other girls; Tammy was tall, slim, with mosquito bites for breast, and nappy hair that was always in a ponytail. On the other hand, Terrance was a cutie. His caramel brown skin tone, light brown eyes, pretty curly hair, and big boy attitude; always made girls look at him twice. But once they noticed his intellect, regular hand-me-downs, Goodwill clothes, and dirty sneakers, his cute smile didn't mean a thing to them.

Now that Tammy was eighteen and a high school graduate, Ms. Betty (Terrance's mother) agreed to let Tammy stay at her home for the next two weeks until she and Terrance left for the military. It was just her way of giving Tammy a chance to wake up in a normal environment with breakfast, prayer, and family. Ms. Betty loved Tammy just as she was her own daughter. She'd always wanted to adopt Tammy but she could barely afford to take care of Terrance off her nursing assistant income.

***

Terrance became great at saving his money from the different jobs he did around the neighborhood. So, he was excited to take Tammy to the state fair before they both left for the military. Tammy seemed down for a few days, so he figured that this would brighten her day.

"Hey, you got plans today?" Terrance asked as he walked into his room that he'd given up to Tammy to make her stay comfortable.

"Hey. I didn't hear you come in," Tammy started to laugh.

"Why you laughing?" Terrance looked down at his work clothes.

"Oh my God! Look at you! You have sheetrock everywhere. If I didn't hear your voice, I wouldn't have known who you were," Tammy teased Terrance as he grabbed some clothes to take a shower.

"Whatever man! I'm tired as hell too! But I still want us to kick it before we leave next week. So what you got going on tonight?" Terrance asked Tammy again as he walked towards the door.

"Really nigga! Damn right we rolling out!" Tammy jumped up off the bed to find some clothes to wear.

"You don't even know where we going? But your fast ass ready to *roll out!*" Terrance teased. "We're going to the state fair. So, I don't think you need to wear your newest *hot* outfit. Terrance emphasized the word "hot" because he knew that any outfit that was new with a tag on it; Tammy and her fake friends had stolen it.

Tammy threw the shirt at Terrance, "Uh-uh! Don't be trying to knock my hustle and flow."

"Looking at this ugly ass shirt it's more like your find and glow 'cause that shirt bright as hell," Terrance said quickly and ran before Tammy threw another shirt at him.

***

They went to the fair and they had a blast. Terrance tried to win every stuffed animal possible for Tammy. He paid for them both to get hand stamps which allowed them to ride all of the rides. Once they made it back to the house, Ms. Betty was already gone to cover her 11pm-7am shift at the nursing home. The both of them were still hyped from the fair and laughing about the fight that broke out afterward.

"Yo! I can't believe Alyssa slapped the shit outta that college chick like that! I mean that shit sounded off! Tammy laughed as her and Terrance walked inside the house and turned on the lights.

She tried to reenact how the slap went but she accidentally slapped Terrance as he was walking by.

"Oh my God! I'm so sorry Terrance," Tammy grabbed his face. "Did it hurt?"

Terrance looked at her crazy, "Hell yeah that hurt! Damn woman!"

They both laughed, which faded into a passionate ten-second kiss. Terrance held Tammy's hand on his face and kissed it. He then grabbed her face with both his hands and they kissed again.

Terrance ran off to the bathroom ashamed of his instant erection that he was sure that Tammy felt. Tammy knocked on the door a few minutes but decided that she would let him come out and talk about his erection on his own time. So she went into the room, changed into her nightgown, and laid in bed staring at the ceiling. She often wondered what sex felt like. She heard all the girls around the way talk about it but most boys weren't checking for her.

She sat up straight in the middle of the bed when she heard Terrance open the bathroom door. He walked to the bedroom door and stood there.

"I want to apologize. I shouldn't have...," Tammy held her head down and placed up her hand.

"I kissed you too! So don't apologize. But can I ask you something?"

"Sure."

Terrance walked over to the bed and sat down. They both played with their fingers scarred to talk about what had just happened Tammy broke the ice.

"We always talk about everything, so I wanna know...," Tammy paused as she looked down at her hands. "...Have you ever did *it* before?"

"Oh hell yeah! I gets my mack on."

Tammy knew he was lying. She started laughing, "Nigga you are lying your ass off!"

She continued to laugh but before she knew it, Terrance was kissing her again. Once she didn't stop him, it wasn't long before Terrance was on top of Tammy.

He kissed her as if he had been kissing her for years, he held nothing back. Moving down to her small breast, grabbing a handful of them he sucked them both. Tammy removed her nightgown completely revealing her small frame. She helped Terrance remove his clothes and his penis was standing tall; looking at his size made her a little nervous.

Terrance started to kiss her again, "What should I do next?"

"I don't know I guess just put it in."

Terrance used his fingers to guide his penis into Tammy's opening. She was so tight and he was so large, it was a painful and pleasurable thing. Tammy squirmed, ouched from his thickness entering her tightness, and moaned as Terrance made his way deeper into her virginity. But once he was inside her, it was over within minutes, and Tammy was glad.

They laid there quiet for a few seconds. Terrance didn't know what to do next so he decided to do what he felt like doing; kissing Tammy again. But as soon as he turned to kiss her again, she got up, grabbed her nightgown off the floor, and quickly moved to the bathroom and started a hot bubble bath. Tammy stayed inside the bathroom over forty-five minutes; Terrance knocked on the door just as long.

"Tammy, I'm sorry if I hurt you! Tammy! Are you okay?"

Tammy ignored him. She finally came out the bathroom and she thought Terrance would be asleep but he was sitting on the hallway floor. He quickly jumped to his feet.

"Look. I'm sorry. I shouldn't have pushed you. I just was…," Tammy stopped him.

"Terrance. We both did it together. It did hurt. But I think its pose to hurt. Let's just forget about it and move on," Tammy's words cut him deeply.

He looked down at the floor; hurt, ashamed, and confused.

"Okay. I just thought I hurt you because the blood. I changed the sheets on the bed for you."

"I think that's normal too. That's why it's called popping the cherry," they both burst into laughter.

They both spent the night thinking about what they'd just done and how it was going to affect their friendship.

***

Years went by without Tammy and Terrance speaking. They both went to war in Iraq in 2001. Tammy was discharged because she crashed her plane into a village of women and children that died instantly and was injured badly. She was nurtured back to health by one of her sergeants that was discharged with injuries as well. They eventually got married, moved into her husband's apartment building, which he owned in the Bronx, lived; just not happily ever after. He was abusive and a heavy cocaine user. Cocaine eventually moved on to be a habit of how Tammy dealt with her screwed up life. She was diagnosed almost a year after being discharged with post-traumatic stress disorder.

Things took another turn for the worse when her husband died from an overdose on top of her. Even though he was the second person she'd had sex with, she hated having sex with him. She became upset for the way her life was turning out. She was left with this raggedy apartment building, which she now owned, in the worse neighborhood in New York and she just wanted to be free.

One night she ended up selling herself to one of the known drug dealers inside her building. She had no money until the first of the month. And usually once that arrived she was broke again before the middle of the month.

The sex from the drug dealer began to happen more and more often. Quinton was his name and he loved to lace his weed with cocaine. That became another habit she couldn't afford over time. Quinton didn't have much to offer other than lessons on riding his dick late nights but he liked Tammy a lot.

"Look in the mirror? Tell me what you see?" Quinton asked her one night.

"I see a coke head, ugly, country, stupid ass bitch that can't get her shit together. But I know I have the fight in me to do it. I just wish I had my best friend to push me," Tammy said looking down at the floor.

"If you see all that fucked up shit you say you see, well own that shit and be happy about it. You think these crackhead bitches walking around here give a fuck about what motherfuckers think. Fuck No! You always getting high and riding this dick but you not happy so why the fuck you do it if it's not what you wanna do? You, not a dumb ass bitch, like these hoes walking around here. You maybe not the cutest but I've seen some ugly bitches. Maybe you should fix yourself up a little. Check into a rehab for a minute. I don't know. But you just seem too good for this type shit," Quinton said as he stood behind her in the mirror.

Tammy stood holding back her tears because even though Quinton spoke in a harsh tone, he was as sincere as he knew how, and he was speaking the truth. However, when dealing with people who weren't ready to hear the truth, it made them weaker. So later that night Tammy brought some heroine from a fifteen-year-old dealer in her building; she was trying to escape her all of her pain. She felt like she always lost everything close to her. Quinton was getting ready to serve time, she'd lost her mother, her best friend, her career in the air force, her husband, and she felt as if she was losing her mind.

***

It was Sunday, February 10, 2008, at 7:52 a.m. Tammy was sitting in the North Central Bronx Hospital. She'd overdosed on heroin and was in a coma for a few days. She was just waking up and all she could do was cry because she was *still* alive. She didn't have anybody to call so she called Quinton's cell phone only to be told by the little fifteen-year-old boy that he would be running the block because the NARCS picked Quinton up last night. She cried some more but then she picked up the phone again. She was in shock that she still remembered the number after all these years. Her palms started to sweat as the phone continued to ring in her hand.

"Hello." The older lady said softly.

Tammy hesitated for a minute, "Hello, Ms. Betty."

"OH MY GOD! TAMMY! IS THAT YOU?"

"Yes, mam. How are you?" Tammy said with a smirk.

"My sweet Jesus! Baby, you left and never returned. I thought you got killed in the war but Terrance looked it up and you were discharged. We just figured you moved on with your life and forgotten about us," Ms. Betty cried tears of joy. Finally finding out Tammy was alive.

"He did?" Tammy asked.

"Yes. Baby, you knew how my son and I felt about you. Oh, that boy waited on you forever to return to him," Ms. Betty paused. "I feel bad because after seeing him sit in misery for so long, I convinced him to pick his self up and move on. So he did."

"He did?" Tammy half a smile dropped.

"Yes. Baby Terrance has been married and living in Charleston now for about four years. It's so beautiful out there."

"Oh, that's good Ms. Betty. I'm happy for him."

"Are you okay, Tammy? You sound down."

"Yes, mam. I just wanted to call to hear your voice. I'm glad everybody is doing ok."

"Please keep in contact, baby."

"Okay, yes mam. I will keep in touch," tears started to form in Tammy's eyes.

"Wait baby? Did you ever get married?" Ms. Betty asked out of curiosity.

Tammy take a big swallow not wanting to think about her life and how it turned out, "Yes mam. I did. But my husband passed away last year."

"Oh goodness. I'm sorry dear."

"Don't be. I'm not!" Tammy said with a frown. But before Ms. Betty could ask another question, Tammy hurried her off the phone so she could cry her eyes out in silence.

"Okay, Ms. Betty. I gotta go."

"Okay, Tammy. Baby, you sure you are alright?" Ms. Betty asked.

"Yes, I'm fine. I'll talk you later Ms. Betty. I love you!"

"I love you too."

They ended the called. But Tammy's heart broke knowing that she hurt the one person that loved her unconditionally. She never forgot about Terrance and apparently he never forgot her either. But he was married and happy and she wanted him to stay that way.

***

February 15, 2008

Tammy was sitting in her half-empty apartment on her birthday. With no friends, no family, and not much

166

money to buy anything, she decided that she would order Chinese takeout and watch bootleg DVDs all day. She was released a day after she talked to Ms. Betty on the phone. Since then she decided that she was gone stay clean of drugs. Even though it was just two weeks, Tammy smiled looking at her clean face and five pounds that she'd gain during her hospital stay.

She was just starting to watch Poetic Justice when a knock came to the door. She figured it was one of the apartment building dealers trying to see if she wanted to buy a hit.

"GO AWAY!" Tammy yelled from the chair.

But the knock continued and whoever it was became persistent. She got up, walked to the door, and looked out the peep hole but they had it covered. Her mind went to it being Quinton but she knew that couldn't be true. So she just opened the door.

"Hello, Tammy. I'm sorry for just showing up to your home like this but I just had to see for myself that you were okay?"

Tammy stood with tears falling down her cheeks; speechless.

"Well, could I come in for a minute? Also, could you please get these two dozen roses before I drop them? Being that, I had to walk ten flights of stairs. Your elevators are out!"

Tammy grabbed the roses, placed them on the table right behind her, and turned to take another look, "How did you find me?"

"Really, Tammy? The world is run by the internet. Once momma said you called from a hospital in the Bronx, I looked your ass up."

"Terrance!" Tammy cried as she hugged him tightly.

But that tight hug turned into the same passionate kiss they shared eight years ago.

"No! No! No! Wait! I'm sorry. You're a married man now," Tammy said wiping her mouth and then his. "I'm just glad you're here."

"Tammy, I'm getting a divorce."

Her eyes widen, "WHAT? Why? You're still considered newlyweds. Tammy went to sit back down on the couch as she led Terrance in hand behind her.

He looked down at the floor but quickly back up at Tammy, "Well for starters, look what just happened?" He grabbed Tammy's hand and rubbed his slightly harden penis with it.

Tammy laughed and blushed as she playfully slapped Terrance on the shoulder, "You so nasty."

"Nah, but on some real, I'm getting a divorce because I don't have who I want. I've been in love with you since the day I saw you at that bus stop," Terrance paused closing his eyes for a second reminiscing about the night they shared.

"And that night we shared before we left, I never stopped thinking about it. Tammy, I did everything as we were young how I felt every King should've treated his queen. I didn't have much. But I always wanted to give you so much more."

Terrance got down on one knee; he took the ring box from his pocket and continued to speak.

"Tammy Evonne Groves, I'm getting a divorce because the woman I should've married and never let leave my side is still alive. I thought you were gone forever. But when my momma told me you called and that your husband died. I knew I had a fighting chance."

Tammy still cried, "No! Terrance, you have a happy life. You can't just leave your wife because of me."

"Tammy you are not listening, I've never hid the fact that you were the love of my life from her. She said to me that if I was to come find you we would be over because I wouldn't need her anymore and she was right," a tear drop fell from Terrance's eye.

"I'm prepared to walk away without you. But I wanted to ask you to become my wife on your birthday and I wanted you to become my wife on my birthday on the 17th."

"So will you marry me?"

Tammy wiped his tears from his eyes. She got down on her knees as well.

"Terrance I never understood why you always was so kind to me. I never understood you not dating any other girls when we were younger. You turned my world around that day at the bus stop. I was stupid because I left behind the one person that had the ability to turn my hurt into happy. I've been hurting for eight years without you by my side and today you've turned that all around. So, I will not have wasted any more of your time…," Tammy stood to her feet and Terrance quickly stood to his even though he was afraid to see where she was going with this.

"I'm saying yes to being your best friend, your lover, and wife on my birthday and yes to becoming your wife on the 17th!"

Tammy and Terrance kissed, shared a hug, and jumped up and down just as they did on their graduation day.

"And that monster most stay put until the night of the 17th," Tammy teased.

"I can handle that as long as I get to put this monster inside you for the rest of my life!"

Phylicia began her love for writing as a child. Writing was an outlet for her; however, it was her first career choice.

Phylicia enjoyed working in the medical field, but quickly put that on hold to be a stay-at-home mom. During that time, she refocused her attention on her writing and *Carolina Rich* was born. Now with four completed manuscripts, a featured short story in Niyah Moore's *Patron on Ice* anthology and her *Sexrotica Diaries Blog*, she's only getting started on her journey to becoming a great author. For more information on Phylicia, check out her website: www.AuthorPhyliciaG.com

ACT IV:

DRAMATIC

LOVE

Distractions

Kaylynn Hunt

"Love me or hate me, both are in my favor…If you love me, I'll always be in your heart…If you hate me, I'll always be in your mind."

-William Shakespeare

The Things I Get Myself Into

"Damn! Four dicks in three days but only one crossed these lips." My past weekend reminded me of what I call the "good ole days". Honestly, I had to have a conversation with myself, after all, was said and done. Nothing about my life has ever been socially acceptable or conventional but I've accepted myself. I can't tell everyone my "real" life or they'd be looking down their noses at me. However, I'm who I am and don't really give a fuck what people think about me. I don't think I could narrow down where my 'good ole times' went downhill.

There seemed to be one thing after another and frankly, my patience had run the fuck out.

Perez, my most prized stallion, either paid a little too much attention to me or I paid too much attention to him. People began to talk about how much time Perez and I spent together. So, I tried getting with other people to keep down confusion. When I went back to getting what I wanted, it became a problem. Basically, they're fighting over me. It was too much and I had to cut Perez off. I'm telling you all of this under the assumption that you know the dynamics of the swinger lifestyle. That's how I found my stallion...

Let me explain things a little better for you. I'll start with, yes black people swing. I have never had any pink meat and don't find it too appealing at this time. But I digress, parties.... You don't just walk into a room and start fucking. I guess you could and that is kind of what I did. However, that's not really how it goes down. Mainly couples; married, engaged or whatever come out to meet other couples or singles that they wouldn't mind sharing their partners with. Generally, there is a meet and greet to get to know who you're dealing with then get it in as you feel. With some people, it's easier than others and each day is hit or miss.

In my case, I'm a single female, a hot commodity in this circle, especially adding the fact that (not tooting my own horn) I'm fine and sexy as hell. I'm going to admit couples were coming at me left and right. Damn near all of them trying to get a piece of this pie. After I got with Perez, I really wasn't checking for anyone else. I had already got the dick I liked. Therefore, there was no need to keep looking. Why rock the boat? Don't get me wrong, I wasn't staking a claim or anything. That nigga continued to fuck any and every one he wanted. As long as I got mine by the end of the night I was cool. Sometimes, I started my night out making sure I got it first because I didn't want to go behind anyone or wait in line. Not that I ever had to wait in line, when I said I was ready, I got it. Why fuck around and get some shit I didn't like? I knew exactly where to get what I wanted and how I wanted it.

Believe me, I tried, by testing out a few others in the fold. They were good but no Perez. More than just the dick and the fucking, we had this weird energy. Chemistry is a muthafucka; our pheromones must have been a perfect mixture. I realize even in this environment the appearance of us ALWAYS being seen together might seem a little suspicious but, when someone has the nerve to speak on it then it becomes a problem.

Here's what happened: Sara, one of my swinger friends, invited a few of us out for her man, Terrence's birthday. It was maybe four couples, one of Sara's girlfriends and little ole me. We went to see some strippers, get some drinks then went back to Sara's. We drunk some more, smoked weed, listened to music, yada, yada, yada, you get the point. Drink + me = fucking, that's just the way it is. So, Perez and I slip off to a bedroom and do what we do best. Some other things went on here and there. Ends up, I'm in the bed sleeping with Sasha (Perez's wife) and here comes Sara.

"How dare you not give Terrence some? You came out for HIS birthday and you can't even fuck him?"

I just looked at her and laughed because surely she's kidding. She said something to Sasha. I don't even remember what it was but, I just went back to sleep. I had an early morning event and thought nothing else of it. Now, I want you to understand that Sara called me two days prior to this asking me to make sure to tell Perez to come because she had talked to Sasha and wasn't sure if they were coming. As she explained if I told him to come then she knew that they would. Now, if she had a problem with me fucking him, then she shouldn't have made sure he was there. But, who the hell said I was obligated to fuck her man? I do who and what I want and just because we hang out, you're cool and I'll laugh with you doesn't mean I have to fuck you.

I thought nothing of Sara's mini bitch fit. I later found out that she made it a point to shine light on Perez and I's activities to Sasha, which caused drama. She must not realize that she'd ruined that occasional romp.

Terrence, nor would she ever taste this pussy again. Hating ass bitch!

And that's when I said good-bye to the "good ole days". Today is something different altogether. Perez and I haven't fucked in quite some time. It's hit and miss at best when I'm at my most desperate point due to a lack of sexual satisfaction. I have a list of "go throughs" to keep my attitude in check. *I really think I have a problem.* There is this one guy I like but he travels a lot. If he even hinted that he wanted more, I'd bite. But he hasn't. So, I'll keep Shawn to what he offers, some conversation, dates occasionally, great sex, a few drinks, and laughs when he has the time. Let me tell you about Shawn's ass, he is a successful small businessman and sexy. He is everything any girl could want but a bachelor all the same. I really shouldn't have been fucking with him to begin with because mixing business with pleasure leads to disaster. Wait did I even tell you my name? It's Savannah. If you haven't already guessed. This isn't your typical love story.

How things changed

Back to my current situation, since I'd cut Perez off, my pickings were slim. I could be too particular sometimes and ended up going without until I could get what I wanted. Do you know what happens when you deprive an addict of their addiction then hand feed it to them? They binge. I've been kind of incognito for a few months. A few of my old "regulars" had been hitting me up and I would blow them off. I wouldn't admit it to myself but I was really just wanting one man but had too much pride to just fucking say the shit. Nonetheless, a horny demon will overrule anything when at its limit. I needed a distraction before I gave into this nagging feeling of, dare I say, infatuation. I'd decided I was "getting it in" all weekend but I wasn't having muthafuckas running in and out my house. I rented a room in downtown Detroit to enjoy having some fun.

First up was this dude named John (#2), he and I had not yet had the pleasures but I was looking forward to calling him on his head game. We met through a mutual friend and had been chatting for some time via text and or messenger. John boasted very proudly of his expertise in oral satisfaction. It intrigued me quite a bit. Though, I think I get more lasting pleasure from penetration. However, I would never turn away great cunnilingus. I'm spoiled in that way, come with top notch both or I'll pass on the next time. I'd let John know that I'd be free for the evening. There was an errand or two I needed to run but I'd let him know when I was done. He worked afternoons so it was cool with his schedule since he got off at ten pm.

I got kind of tied up during my last errand and I didn't try to contact him until after midnight. By kind of tied up, I mean I ran into this dude Oscar (#4) I used to see when I went out frequently, he bought me a few drinks. We sat and conversed about why I blew him off before. *I really couldn't think of a good reason.* But regardless when I sent a text to John, I got no response. I took that to mean it was too late for him to get away. Now, John and I hadn't discussed his living situation. I'll admit I never asked. However, I got wind that he was living with a not so broken up with ex. Don't get me wrong, I didn't care who he lived with. It was no matter when he didn't respond, I moved on to the next man on the list, Derrick. I met him in the swinger circle. He tried getting at me, halfheartedly (in my opinion) but I paid him no mind. That was until, I just so happened to see a picture of his dick, that muthafucka was impressive. After that, I started responding more often to his sparse "hi's and hello's" in my message box. As a result, I had enough rapport with him to tell him to fall through my hotel room after I'd gotten in there. I refused to waste that night's money.

Derrick (#1) came in with stars in his eyes. Well, I was naked after all, no reason for giving false pretense. First off, he ate my pussy like it was his lunch. I'm sorry if I'm too blunt for you but I'm not the sugar coating kind. Not one inch of my lower regions were left untouched by his tongue. He gave that special attention to my clit that had me leaving his face quite wet. He put that dick in after I came all on his tongue and BA-BY I gasped. He stroked it smoothly, steadily and with purpose. I could feel myself stretch and contract around his shaft. He got extra points for talking to me while he fucked me. Telling me to come on his dick, calling me baby and demanding that I give it to him, just made it worth my while. We or shall I say he probably fucked me 30/40 minutes. Only stopping a couple times in between so I'd cum on his tongue again, so maybe it was an hour. I fell off to sleep right when he got up to flush the condom. Although, I'm usually anticipating a man getting up and getting the hell out I wasn't mad when he woke me up with the tongue before he escorted himself out.

About 30 minutes after Derrick left, John sent a text. I told him where I was, what room and then got in the shower, rinsing that rubber taste out my pussy. *Yeah, yeah, I'm a nasty bitch.* But when he walked in and saw me naked he didn't hesitate to dive face first in this pussy as he'd promised. He did NOT disappoint either. I'd never been in so many positions in one sitting from just getting head. On my back, legs wide open, sideways, doggy-style, riding, and etc. we switched positions like I had a dick in me and I came in every one of them. This went on for at least 40 minutes if not longer. I had to check out at 11 (or so he thought) and we'd exceeded our time. Now that I think about it. I guess we can't consider John a "dick" because I didn't even see it. He never even took his pants off. Dick wasn't on that menu but I was not short on orgasms in the least. I hope you don't feel like I'm rushing through these encounters but I'm trying to get to the good part. YES! It gets better.

When it gets real

Victor (#3), Victor, Victor is the dude that WAS a serious regular but got cut off. In the last few months, he's been in my inbox professing to miss me and want to take me out and etc. Now, we never went out or anything before and part of the reason he got cut off in the first place was he couldn't keep me in his rotation as often as I would have liked. I take that back. There was a time I was seeing him two to three times a week and then something happened with him and he fell off. I just wasn't feeling trying to fit back in after he came back on the scene. Simply because he didn't feel I was important enough to know whatever his issue was when he fell off. I needed to back myself up. I read too much importance into that half a week then there was, obviously.

Anyway, if I couldn't tell you anything else about him I could tell you he was hung like a fucking horse. That is why he was on the agenda. AND I mean literally. But you can probably deduce that the dick had to be good if we used to frequent each other several times a week. In my mind, I knew he'd scratch this itch I have. *No, it was not gone yet.* Let me explain something, with he and I there was some semblance of friendship. We got together, talked, drank, ate together and so on. Which I guess was another reason why I was so put off by the absence of an explanation for the brief disappearance. *I think he got locked up but I never asked for confirmation.* We did much of the same when I saw him. He was a little more touchy-feely than usual. To which I asked,

"You miss me or something?"

"You know I did."

"I don't know shit."

"Let me show you," he said.

Victor slid his arm from around me as we were seated on the couch next to one another. *I had gone to his crib.* He stood in front of me, stretched out his hand to assist me in standing. He led me to the bedroom which was dimly lit with candles and filled with soft music. He tried to be silly and dance a little in the middle of the room. When that was done, he kissed my forehead which took a little dipping down for him since he's 6'2 and I'm 5'4". After which he undressed me slowly, placing kisses in various places as he did so, a shoulder, the nape of my neck, my wrist, a hip; you get the point. Victor walked me over to the bed and pushed me over, I flopped on my back. He dove his head right between my legs. You would've thought my labia were metal and his lips were a magnet or vice versa the way they interlocked. He sucked, flicked, licked and twirled his tongue around and through every part of my vagina. I rocked, bucked, pumped and humped his lips and tongue right back.

He took a step back to come out of his jogging pants and my mouth started watering. That dick was a masterpiece. And it HAD to cross my lips. I knew that dick and I missed it, I didn't realize it until then, how much. I wrapped my hand around it and began to stroke it. My hand wouldn't even close completely around it. My nails didn't even touch. I had to taste it. I HAD to wrap my lips around it and wet it with my tongue. It seemed like a sin not to. I loved hearing him moan when my lips closed around it. The trace of my tongue around that thick vein running up the side made me tingle. I was on my knees on the bed as he stood at the foot paying homage to that beautiful creation then he pushed me off.

"I want that pussy," he said.

He crawled up on the bed with me, grabbed one ankle and when he pushed inside me I thought I was being sent to another planet. I felt every millimeter of skin enter me and it felt like heaven.

"I'm going to show you much I missed this pussy."

He said it and he did it. I was flipped, flopped, thrown to the side, upside down, right side up and ran down through there. You understand me? I could not even begin to tell you how long we went at it. It was way over an hour. By the time it was over the sheets were half off the bed and the part that was left had a wet spot. He had me telling him I missed the dick, loved the dick, wouldn't leave the dick again, give me the dick, save a dick, I'd suck a dick whatever half a sentence popped in my head. I must've fallen asleep as soon as he pulled it out of me. And I woke up in the morning when he turned me over and licked me awake. Lawd, I hadn't been fucked so good in the combination of the two before him. I had plans on returning to that for the night but it didn't happen. And that's where Oscar (#4) comes in. I was out drinking again, met him at the bar. With the realization, I wasn't getting at Victor again for the night following a few text messages I figured I had to fill in my night. Since it couldn't even come close, I won't even bore you with the details. I thought of Victor all night. I didn't even let Oscar spend the night.

"You gotta go."

"You putting me out?" He asked.

"I can't sleep with people. You gotta go."

After little protest, he got his shit and left and I drifted off.

THE AFTERMATH

The problem after putting in work with a dick you couldn't give two shits for is you don't wanna be bothered afterward. Each one of those dudes caught me on the right wave and that was all to it. They distracted me for the weekend and I'd smile at the fond memories but Shawn was still on my mind. From the day I met him, I knew there was something between us but I refused to buy into it. No matter how many men I ran through, they weren't him and I'd never be satisfied. As I sat, thinking about who it was that satisfied me, I almost picked up my phone. Damn! That pride of mine wouldn't let me hit send, though. I busied myself with work. I pushed all the dick and lips out of my mind as I tried to focus on getting ahead of the curve with my event planning.

I was sitting there typing on my computer and I noticed something out the corner of my eye.

"Don't do that. You scared the shit outta me. You can NOT sneak up on me like that," I said as I looked up.

"I apologize. I didn't mean to scare you I was just taking in the beautiful view."

"Stop it with the charm. What's up? Did we have an appointment?"

"No. I was in the neighborhood and I just stopped by to see if you had time for lunch today."

"I'm so glad you thought of me."

"I always do," he said. He always flattered me in that way.

"Shawn, will you cut it out? I think you just like seeing me blush."

"I do."

"Well sir, you picked a good day. I sure would love to join you for lunch."

"Wait. Are we on a time limit?" He asked.

"Actually, my afternoon is wide open. I'm really just here to be here."

"Well, pencil me in for the rest of the afternoon then."

"Give me a minute, I'll be right out."

Shawn walked out of the office and I quietly hyperventilated as I shut my programs down and prepared to leave. What are the odds? Dare I call this fate? I've been trying to distract myself from him, he's been thinking of me. Then began the date that never ended. Who said you can't turn a hoe into a housewife?

Kaylynn produces interesting, captivating and stimulating pieces of work, which absorbs the reader down to the last page. Kaylynn has used not only her imagination, but glimpses of the life she's lived to produce quality, flowing works of art. Living outside the box is something she excels at.

Kaylynn opens you up to things that will make you think beyond the norm.

To read more about Savannah and Shawn check out Catching Dreams by Kaylynn Hunt

For more information about Kaylynn, find her on Facebook at

https://www.facebook.com/KaylynnHunt

Twitter http://twitter.com/savannahw

Website http://www.kaylynnhunt.com/

Say It Ain't So
Ni'Kay Rountree

"Expectation is the root of all heartache."

-William Shakespeare

Chelsea

As much as I wanted to forget everything that has happened to me over the past four years, I knew that I couldn't. Self-reflection can be a bitch, but if you let my therapist tell it—it's necessary for continued growth. The way I see it, I haven't changed much since high school, but I have learned to be on top, you have to think like a boss. In my world, it was all about me, and I made sure that my shit was always tight.

I wore my jet-black hair in a two-strand twist out the majority of the time. My almond-shaped, hazel-brown eyes were my best feature, sometimes giving people the impression that I am of Asian descent. I had to work extra hard to keep my five feet, three-inch body Bally's Health Club figure. My body was so tight, the men in the gym, hell, some of the women too, could barely concentrate on what they were doing. To top it all off, I had the brains to match. With all of those qualities in one woman, it makes you wonder why Anthony, my supposed to be fiancé, strayed. I swear that when it comes to sex, men think with the wrong head. I guess that was the head Anthony was thinking with when he cheated on my ass.

Anthony and I have been dating for almost four years. In 2007, he proposed, but I told his ass, *No.* Anthony wasn't worthy of my hand in marriage. Yes— *worthy.* He cheated on me the year before he proposed. Most of my family and best friend, Asia, thought the only reason he proposed was to make amends for cheating on me with some hood rat he met in the club.

What would cause him to go to the gutter when he had someone like me? Compared to that hood rat, ghetto bitch he was messing with, I was a perfect ten.

As the owner of one of the hottest hair salons in Houston, I made it a point to be a trendsetter. I never was caught slipping. I was at all of the hair shows and kept my models tight. I set the example that I expected my employees to follow. My seven stylists knew the deal. If they didn't fall in line, then they knew exactly where they would be going—out the door. If I could work my way up from the bottom, then so could they. I wouldn't accept anything less.

My clients were some of the top African-American judges, lawyers, doctors, and congresswomen, and men, in town. I even catered to an elite group of R&B and hip-hop artists. My salon brings in a net income of over a million dollars a year. I wish my love life could be as successful as my business. *Damn. I hated self-reflection.*

I reached over to my nightstand, opened the drawer and put my journal back in its place. In my opinion, the only reflection I needed was how to get my man to remain faithful. Dr. Anthony Chadwick was too good of a catch to let some rat move in and take my place. *That was not happening.*

My first appointment was at nine. I knew that if I didn't get up and hit the shower, I was going to be late. Tardiness was my pet peeve. All of my stylists knew it too. They found out how serious I was when they watched me fire Shatina as soon as she stepped foot in the door. Her client had been waiting for two hours by the time she showed up. I didn't care she had kids and barely made her rent every month. I had a brand to protect. If you are messing with my brand, then you are messing with my money, and she had to go.

As I hopped in the shower, I began to come alive as the water beaded up on my skin. As I continued to lather my body with my sponge, I realized Anthony hadn't called me back. I finished my shower, wrapped my towel—embroidered with my initials—around my body, and checked the clock to see how much time I had left before I needed to leave for work.

I dressed in a pair of white Capris and a black crop top. I threw on my black, Jimmy Choo sandals and headed for the kitchen. I gulped down my chocolate breakfast shake, grabbed my keys and walked out of the door to get into my Lexus GS 500.

Dang it! I left my phone—my lifeline.

I turned and made a beeline back to the front door. As soon as I opened the door, I could hear my phone ringing. I picked up my stride to catch it before the caller hung up. Once I reached the kitchen counter, I could see Anthony's picture on my screen.

"Hello," I said.

"Hey sugar," Anthony replied.

"Hey Ant," I said, in a hostile tone.

Anthony gasped. I assume he was shocked by my nonchalant greeting; however, if he thought I had forgotten that I didn't get a call back last night, he was crazy. Although I had forgiven Anthony for cheating on me, I didn't have amnesia. I continued to remain suspicious of him. I was borderline obsessed. My friend Asia often joked about my stalker-like tendencies.

"Chelsea, I wanted to call and let you know I love you," Anthony said.

"Why didn't you call me back last night?" I exclaimed.

"Babe, my phone was dead. I left my charger at home on the nightstand. I am sorry, baby. I didn't mean to have you worried," he apologized.

"Well, I don't see why you couldn't call me from the hospital. Don't they have a phone? Don't they have several phones?"

I realized that Anthony seemed to get a little perturbed by my negativity when he said, "Look, Chelsea, I told you I am sorry. I told you what happened. What else do you want me to fucking say?" He yelled. "This shit is starting to get old."

Although every bit of my being believed he was lying, I had no proof, so I said, "Look, Ant, I'm sorry. I don't want to argue. I can't help I worry about you. Call me from the hospital the next time to let me know you are

199

okay. I have to get to work. I will call you later. I love you. Goodbye." I clicked the End button.

"I can't keep doing this to myself. I have to get a grip," I said out loud as I popped a Xanax in my mouth and swallowed it dry. *This shit is getting ridiculous.* My insecurities were driving me crazy.

***

It usually took less than thirty minutes for me to get to work, except when there was traffic on Interstate 610. The less than thirty-minute drive turned into over an hour commute due to the stop and go traffic because of the commuters from the outskirts of Houston were trying to get into the city for work. I regretted not taking the metro to downtown. The traffic simply made for a frustrating start to my already frazzled morning.

I must calm my nerves. I reached over to my radio dial and turned to 99.7 FM, one of Houston's hottest jazz stations.

As I hit the button on the steering wheel to turn up the volume, I stopped and flipped off the dumbass who almost hit my car while trying to squeeze his huge Tahoe in front of my Lexus.

"Yes, I have road rage, you son of a bitch!" I yelled.

As I started to calm down, I heard a familiar voice on the radio.

Hey, Houston, it's your boy Sweet Rick Staton. I am here for one night only at the Love Jones Comedy Club. I will be doing two shows. One will be at 8 p.m. and, the other at 10 p.m. Come on out and get some laughs. The first five ladies at each show will receive an autographed copy of my stand up video."

Oh, my goodness—Ricky? What in the world—a comedian! Go figure.

I hadn't seen Rick since we dated in college. We met at Prairie View A&M University. He was a mass communications major, and I studied social work. He asked me out several times before I agreed to dinner and a movie.

The night he came to pick me up, I was surprised. He drove his dad's crimson colored Beamer. As I approached the bottom of the stairwell, I could see Ricky and Asia talking at the front desk. He had on blue dress pants and a blue and white striped shirt, which he left open at the top to show his fraternity brand. He looked delicious as he stood there in the fluorescent lighting of the dorm's main lobby. To complement his glowing caramel complexion, he had a low haircut with the edges sharp, and a goatee with the chin strap going up the side of his face.

"Well, hey there, Chelsea! You look… um, um good," he stated, as he licked his sexy lips. The girls in the lobby had no shame as they continued to hang around and gaze at Ricky.

"You look good yourself and thank you," I said, making sure I bit the bottom of my lip to tease him a little.

"I am certain my dorm mates agree," I said, giving the gazing girls the evil eye. *Vulture bitches.*

Ricky presented me with a dozen pink roses. No guy had ever done this before, especially on a first date. As he gave me the roses, he gently kissed me on the cheek, and chills shot through my body like an electrical shock. I was genuinely impressed. "Are you ready?" he asked, offering me his arm.

Ricky and I became friends, lovers, and soulmates. Our love affair lasted my entire junior year. Ricky graduated and left to complete an internship at a radio station in Atlanta, Georgia. We attempted the long distance thing; however, it was too much of a strain, and we both reluctantly ended it.

After hearing his voice on the radio, I knew tonight's new destination for my birthday was The Love Jones Comedy Club.

Asia

Chelsea finally made it to the shop. I knew she was going to pitch a bitch when she noticed that someone had parked in her parking space.

"Okay y'all, I see her pulling up. You already know she is going to walk up in here tripping, so just act like you don't know what the hell she is talking about," I said.

When Chelsea walked in her face was twisted. She was mad as hell.

"Hey, Chels," I said casually and continued to press my client's hair.

"What's up everybody? Do any of you know who parked in my parking space?" Chelsea asked.

No one spoke up.

"Hey, does the cat have everybody's tongue? Hello-ooo. Can you all hear me?"

She flailed her hands as if she were doing sign language or something.

"Who the hell is parked in my parking space?" Chelsea's forehead had a wrinkle in it, which usually occurred just before she knocked somebody upside the head.

I watched her as she walked towards the back of the salon and posed the question to each of the ladies seated under a dryer. *Poor ladies.*

Just as I instructed, no one mumbled a word.

"You know what, since the cat has *everybody's* tongue, I am going to call the police and have the car towed. Do any of you want to speak up now?" She stood with her left hand on her hip and held her cell in the other.

"Damn Chelsea. I told them not to say anything to you, but the car is yours. Anthony and his homeboy, Todd, stopped by early this morning. Ant said it is an early birthday present and wanted to surprise you," I screamed across the salon.

As expected, Chelsea walked over to my booth with a smile on her face. It was more like a foot in her mouth.

"Crazy girl— Anthony told me to tell you to call him when you get here," I told her.

"Asia. I hate you! You know I hate surprises. How many times do I have to tell you that?"

She hugged and kissed me on the cheek.

"Oh my God. I can't believe I acted like an ass—and you let me. I feel so stupid. As a matter of fact, I treated Ant so wrong this morning when he called," Chelsea shared. "Where are the keys, Asia?"

I grabbed the key out of my booth drawer and threw it to her and said, "Yeah. You did act like a bit of an ass."

I still couldn't believe that Anthony bought that girl a brand new red, C250 Mercedes Benz.

Chelsea

I couldn't believe Anthony got me my dream car for my thirtieth birthday. I was so excited that I grabbed the keys from Asia and went outside to check it out. *I got me a Mercedes!*

I couldn't stop smiling. After playing with some of the features for about fifteen minutes, I locked the doors, ran back into the salon, and told Angel, the receptionist, to reschedule all of my appointments for Saturday after 10 a.m. I grabbed my Michael Kors purse and ran out the door. I moved my Mercedes in front of the salon, jumped into my now spare car, the Lexus, and parked it in my reserved space, and then I ran back into the salon.

"Asia, can you do me a favor and work out a plan to get the Lex to my house? Try to get it done early enough so we won't be late for our girl's night out."

Asia looked at me but didn't respond.

"By the way, I changed my mind about the Aqua Lounge. I want to go to the comedy club. Thanks, sweetie. Bye!" I barked. *I didn't have time for Asia's hating ass. I was out!*

I jumped back into my Mercedes and headed to Anthony's job. I had to thank him in person!

Asia

By 7:00 p.m., I still had not made it to Chelsea's place with her car. She had called my phone six times. I didn't answer.

When I finally arrived at Chelsea's house about 7:45 p.m., her impatient ass was waiting for me on the porch. She wore an all-black catsuit adorned with gold accessories. Her black and gold Coach bag and shoes complemented her outfit well. You could tell she hit the gym on a regular. Her developing six-pack peeked through her catsuit. I definitely could not compete. I stopped trying.

"You look cute soror," I said. "Sorry it took me so long, but I had a hard time finding someone to help me out with your car. Thank goodness for Stevie!"

"Great! Remind me to give him a cookie on Monday. Can we go now?" She demanded.

She was such a freaking bitch—line sister or not.

"Okay. We can go. Here are your keys," I said as I tossed them to her.

She caught them and exclaimed, "Oh no! I'm not driving. It's *my* birthday weekend. You're driving my car!"

She tossed the keys back, and we headed to the Love Jones Comedy Club.

Like I said—Bitch.

***

We arrived at the club at 8:05 p.m. I could see the line as we pulled into the parking lot. *Shit, I know I am about to hear her mouth.*

"See, if we would have gotten here earlier, we could have received the free DVD," she complained.

"If you would have taken care of your own damn cars, then maybe I would have been on time," I mumbled.

"Excuse me. I didn't hear you," she said. "Do you mind repeating yourself?"

"Let's park so we can get in line before they sell out," I said abruptly, cutting her off.

Before getting out of the car, Chelsea checked her makeup for the tenth time. She reached into her purse and refreshed her hot spots with her travel size, spray bottle of Chanel No. 9.

"Want some?" She asked.

"No. I'm good. I have on my Juicy. Come on. Let's go. I thought you were in a hurry."

Chelsea led the way, of course. We walked towards the club and fell in line. It took about five minutes to get up to the bouncers. They checked our identification and bags before we entered.

"We have to get a seat in the front," she said, pulling my hand as she pushed a path through the people searching for seats.

"Wait a minute. I am not sitting in the front row at a comedy show. Are you crazy?"

"I have to be in the front. I want Rick to know I'm here. It's my birthday, Asia. Can you please just make an exception?" She pointed at a table for two in front of the stage.

I realized we could touch the stage if we sat there, but we sat down anyway. I immediately ordered my first drink, a Long Island Ice Tea.

"I am so glad drinks are half off, because I am going to need several of these to keep my cool if someone cracks one joke on me while I am sitting this close to the damn stage!" I complained. *Ugh. Chelsea is such a selfish bitch.*

I started to sip on my second glass of Long Island when the music softened, and the lights began to dim. The MC came to the stage.

After a couple of wacky jokes, he finally said,

"Without further delay, The Love Jones Comedy Club presents, Sweet Rick Staton!"

The crowd erupted in applause. Chelsea couldn't keep still. She moved back and forth in her seat so fast; I thought she was going to have an orgasm.

"Here he comes, Asia." Chelsea started licking her lips.

What in the hell. . . I just looked at her.

Rick walked on the stage, and then my mouth dropped.

"Shit! He is still *fine!*" I shouted. Chelsea threw a dagger look at me. "He is," I responded.

"Hooouston! What is going on? I see you up in the house and looking good tonight," Rick commended the audience.

Rick started his show, and he was hilarious. In between his sips of water, I would glance over at Chelsea. She clung to every word that came out of his mouth. I could tell Rick was cognizant of her presence in the audience. He seemed to give our table a lot of eye attention whenever he addressed the audience. I prepared for a long night.

After Rick had ended his show, we made some small talk.

"Chelsea, I hoped you and your friend would stick around," he said as he gave me the once over. "Asia. Right?"

I smiled. I was surprised he remembered me. "Hey, Rick. I enjoyed your show."

"Yeah, Rick. I enjoyed it too," Chelsea repeated. She looked at me like *back off bitch*.

I could not understand why Chelsea started acting so crazy. *It's not as if she doesn't have a man at home.* I stood back and watched Chelsea as she pushed herself up on Ricky—literally.

"So, what do y'all have planned for the rest of the night?" Rick asked.

"Absolutely nothing. What's up?" Chelsea said.

"Well, I'm having an after party at my hotel. I want you ladies to join me," he said.

"We're down," Chelsea answered, cutting her eyes at me in an attempt to read my expression.

"It's settled. I will see you, ladies, there. I'm at the Embassy Suites on Main Street, Room 1012."

Chelsea

I knew Asia didn't want to go to the after party, but I didn't give a shit. It was my birthday, and she was coming along for the ride if she wanted to or not. *She is so damn selfish at times!*

We arrived at the Embassy Suites and parked in the garage. I noticed Asia made it a point to reapply her makeup and perfume. *Why in the hell is she freshening up?*

"Asia, I hope you don't get mad at me, but what are you doing?" I asked.

"Well, I'm getting right. Remember, I don't have a man. . . You do," she snapped.

Oh no, she didn't go there.

"Look, I love Anthony, but what I have learned over the past couple of years is that I have to look out for me! Plus, he isn't the only one who can play the game. The only difference is I'm smart enough not to get caught!" I schooled her.

"Well, I hope you're prepared for the consequences. Men aren't as accepting as women when it comes to infidelity," she responded.

"Shut up Asia," I shouted.

I got out of the car and started walking to the elevator. Asia reluctantly followed.

We were quiet as the elevator carried us up to the main lobby. It was kind of awkward. We walked over to the main elevator and made our way to the tenth floor.

"Room 1012 is around the corner," I pointed out when the elevator doors opened. You could hear the music playing half way down the hallway.

We knocked, and a burly man answered the door. Security—maybe?

"Ladies, may I help you?" the bouncer looking man asked.

"Yes, I am Chelsea, and this is my friend, Asia," I responded. "We are guests of Rick."

The bouncer announced our names to someone in the room. We heard a voice say, "Let them in."

He opened the door, and we saw Rick and several other people standing near the wet bar. Others were making small talk in other areas of the room. Rick walked over towards us.

"Glad y'all made it. What can I get you ladies to drink?"

"A coke for me," Asia said.

"That's all. Come on, sweetness. Let me get you something more potent," Rick flirted.

"Rick, I know you have gin and juice." I quickly cut across them. "You know gin will make you sin." I giggled as I rubbed his shoulder.

"No, Rick. I'll take the Coke." Asia cut back across me. *What in the hell? This bitch obviously had too much to drink at the club because she is tripping right now!*

Rick left and stayed for a minute, but he finally returned with our drinks. For the next several hours, we sat around and caught up on each other's lives. We were in utter shock when Rick started to explain that he wasn't single, but had a partner. My face just dropped. I couldn't believe his ass was gay. Then, we heard a knock at the door. I was glad. I didn't want to hear any damn more. As a matter of fact, I was ready to go.

"That's probably my partner now," Rick said as he watched as the bouncer guy opened the door.

The huge doorman was blocking us from seeing Rick's special friend. Rick got up from the couch and walked over to his partner. The bodyguard stepped out of the way, and Rick said, "Ladies. Meet Anthony. My partner."

I looked at Asia. Asia looked at me. "Say it ain't so!"

Anthony stood there and looked at me like a deer caught in some headlights.

"This is your lover," I screamed. "My fiancé!"

Anthony immediately started to stutter. "It's not what you think," he tried to explain.

Rick looked at him. "What the fuck you mean it's not what you think? You didn't say that shit last night. Did you?"

Anthony turned and faced Ricky. "Shut the fuck up."

Anthony tried to grab me. "Get your filthy hands off me. It's bad enough that you were cheating on me with a grimy, low-budget hoe, but you had to go and hook up with my ex-boyfriend on the down low." I balled my fist up and swung on Anthony and missed. I did punch the shit out of Ricky—by mistake.

Ricky's sumo wrestler looking bodyguard stepped up to me. He grabbed me by the waist and forced me out of the door. "You a feisty little thing," he said as he slammed the door in my face.

I banged on the door and yelled at the top of my lungs. "Open up this damn door. I will kick this motherfucker in. Open the damn door. Anthony, you bitch!"

I stood on the other side of the door waiting for my best friend to follow suit, but she didn't. She never came. I continued to bang on the door until I was interrupted by two police officers.

"Ma'am. We need you to come with us."

I screamed. "I can't believe you called the fucking cops on me. Asia. Asia. I know you aren't going to let them do this to me."

I walked down the hallway wondering what in the hell just happened. I could hear the two cops as they poked fun at me from behind.

Asia

We couldn't stop laughing. I replayed the video of Chelsea's face when she saw Anthony walk through the door. The look was priceless. All I needed was a bag of popcorn and some Skittles. Chelsea deserved all of that and then some. Karma is a bad, bad bitch. The Bible mentions Karma—well, sort of. "Do unto others as you want others to do unto you," I quoted. That means Karma is a Bitch! She came back to Chelsea in full force.

"I feel kind of bad for doing that to her," Ricky said.

"She deserved it," Anthony responded. "How is she going to try and play me? I know I made mistakes, but damn. You either forgive me or you don't."

When Chelsea tried to be player of the year, she didn't know Ricky and Anthony were friends. Anthony and Ricky met at a mutual friend's bachelor party. He called Anthony and told him how Chelsea was acting at the Comedy show, and it was on from there. Of course, when Ricky texted Anthony and told him what was going down, at the after-party, he was more than willing to sit back and watch it all happen. We continued to look at the video and clown Chelsea's selfish ass.

After watching it for the fifth time, Anthony's phone rang, and he excused himself. I watched as his jaw dropped to the floor and tears began to flow from his eyes. "No," he yelled. When he got off the phone, he hung up, he was barely consolable.

Ricky and I said in unison, "What's wrong?"

"It's Chelsea," he stammered.

"Well--," I giggled. "What about her?"

Anthony bowed his head. "It was her mother who called. Chelsea got into an accident when she left here. Head on collision with a pickup truck. She's dead."

I yelled, "No! Say it ain't so!"

Yeah. That's the way Karma works. She's a sneaky bitch. She turned that shit around real quick.

Do unto others as you would have them do unto you.

Nikki "Ni'Kay" Rountree, a Chesapeake, Virginia native, is the author of I Am She: Woman to Woman, Cash Rules Everything Around Me and The Cheater's Wife series. She is a graduate of Norfolk State University and Old Dominion University. Nikki obtained her Doctorate of Education from Nova Southeastern University in Instructional Leadership.

She is a member of Sigma Gamma Rho Sorority, Incorporated and The Order of the Eastern Star.

Author Ni'Kay has always enjoyed writing and hopes to continue to share her talents with the world. Aside from writing, she loves traveling, and spending time with her husband, Brian and three daughters: Briana, Kimari, and Laniya. For more information about Ni'Kay R. Twitter: http://twitter.com/AuthorNikay

Facebook: http://facebook.com/authornikay Author Ni'Kay
Website: http://authornikay.weebly.com

Instagram: https://instagram.com/authornikay

ACT V:

FINALE

SONNET 18

Shall I compare you to a summer's day?

You are more lovely and more constant:

Rough winds shake the beloved buds of May

And summer is far too short:

At times the sun is too hot,

Or often goes behind the clouds;

And everything beautiful sometime will lose its beauty,

By misfortune or by nature's planned out course.

But your youth shall not fade,

Nor will you lose the beauty that you possess;

Nor will death claim you for his own,

Because in my eternal verse you will live forever.

So long as there are people on this earth,

So long will this poem live on, making you immortal.

ACKNOWLEDGMENTS

First and foremost, I want to say thank-you to everyone that made this project possible. From the mere idea of an anthology to the actual publication of it, I am completely grateful.

I want to personally thank **Niyah Moore** for helping and guiding me through the process of how anthologies work. Even though I am not one of her authors, her kindness and patience were unwavering. Even before this anthology, she was always one to help you if you asked, regardless of what publishing company you were with. I'm glad to be friends with someone as like-minded as myself. Her desire to help others and stand out from the crowd should be celebrated. I celebrate you, Niyah. Thanks for everything.

I also have to thank **Xyla Turner**. Besides being super busy with her own projects, she also found the time to help me in any way, she could. She was there when the process got hard or when I needed that extra boost of motivation. I can write so much about this woman, but I will sum it up with this; Xyla definitely embodies the *giraffe mentality* and makes sure those around her aim higher than turtles. She is the type of friend, you always want in your corner because you know, she will always have your back. Thanks for being there. You know I appreciate you.

An enormous, gigantic, thank you for **Pure Harmony Literary Services (Shatisha Nash)!** This chick rocks in so many ways. When I say, she worked extremely hard on this project, that is an understatement. She went above and beyond her duties as an editor to make my company's first anthology, a success. Because several of my friends were a part of this anthology, I wanted to be as fair as possible and Shatisha helped me completely with that and kept me on track. Her constructive criticism, sometimes blunt attitude, mixed with her kindness and love for stories, was the perfect mixture to get this project completed. Like others, Shatisha kept me on my A-game and worked hard to make this anthology stand apart from the others. Her creative desire to be unique shows throughout this anthology as more than just an editor. Thank you Shatisha for doing a wonderful job and being a great friend.

To Ni'Kay, Anitra, and Terrie, you guys were among the first people that submitted to my anthology. Thanks for believing in me. Your stories all evoked different emotions. I went from shock to joy to sadness. I can only imagine the power if you three did a story together! I see the bond that you guys share and I completely love it. I see the giraffe in all of you guys and I am so lucky to be in the tower with you guys.

Terrie, so many women, will relate to your story and secretly it will give them a peace of mind in knowing that despite their obstacles, they can still find true love.

Anitra, your story broadcast a male character in a different and more positive light. I loved that. You showed us that it's more to our men than being thugs or womanizers. I loved your story. You going have single women everywhere wishing for their own Giani.

Ni'Kay, the way you switched that story up on me, I'm still in shock. You have a lot of potential that you hold back, let it out girl cause you are awesome! Not only did you deliver a powerful story, but you made it real by inserting some Karma in there.

Kaylynn, I absolutely love, love, love, your uniqueness. There are no words to describe that story. It was exquisitely HOTTTTTT! The way your writing eludes the norm is simply amazing. I definitely see a collabo in our future, LOL!

Niyah, so many people, can relate to your story. Your story makes people want to fall in love for the first time or all over again. I can see us doing a collabo one day as well. Especially since we both are out of the box thinkers and love to stand apart from the norm. You don't need me to tell you that you are talented because it shows. So thanks again for being a part of this project. It was such an honor to have you contribute.

Xyla, smh! I don't even know where to begin. When I first read your story, I almost threw my phone away! I was so angry, but not because the story was horrible but because it was AMAZING! I felt every emotion, envisioned every touch. It was like a real-life romance movie. It evoked that feeling that happily ever after fairy tales give you. You are a truly talented author and I'm honored that you were a part of this project.

Last, but definitely not least, **Phylicia.** One of my closest, dearest friends. I've been saying since day one, how talented you are. I'm not psychic but I saw it in you. You have finally embraced that. Your writing is phenomenal and I see the change in it from where you started to now. Your story honestly made me cry and you know I hate to cry! I was so mad at you. I think I called you and told you about it. Anyway, the realness of that story was so powerful. Like Xyla's and Terrie's story, you make the reader feel every emotion. You have a gift and I hope you continue to embrace it. Thanks for being a part of this anthology.

My story in this anthology was my first attempt at an interracial romance. I wrote this story without reading or researching IR Romance. I have read a few IR books, but for this project I just free wrote.

Also, this is my first story without ANY sex in it and I am simply amazed at how great it turned out. Real romance can exist without hardcore, backbreaking sex!! I been married for almost eleven years, so my alter ego comes out in sex scenes, lol (inside joke). Anyway, I stepped out of my norm and I love it. I just hope my fans love it as much as I do, but even if they don't I tried something new and I don't regret it.

The purpose of an anthology is to showcase different authors' writing, but I think it also unites writers. I have formed a bond with each and every one of you and I hope our friendship continues past the publication of this book. You guys made my company's first anthology possible. So, thanks again for everything and as always, **DON'T BE AFRAID TO BE DIFFERENT! #BEXQUISITE IT'S MUCH MORE FUN!**

Patti Doss

www.ingramcontent.com/pod-product-compliance
Lightning Source LLC
Chambersburg PA
CBHW031122030726
47496CB00002BA/655